"I'll arrange the ceremony for Saturday."

Cole continued, "I'll be there with a minister and witnesses—and you'll be there, too, unless you want to start a war you can't possibly win."

"Saturday's too soon!" Gripping the armrests tightly, she half rose.

"No, Jenny." He came around the desk, lifting her the rest of the way and standing her on her feet. "It's too late—five years too late."

She couldn't look at Cole. "But I need time."

"What for? It's settled—and don't even *think* about running away."

"You mean, don't even think about running away with *your son*. It would probably serve your purposes very well if I'd just take off alone, never to be heard from again. Well, I won't!" She brought fisted hands down on his chest for emphasis. "He's my son, too. I'll never give him up!"

Ruth Jean Dale comes from a newspaper family.
She herself was a reporter for years, and her husband
is the editor of a small Southern California daily.
Even her youngest daughter works as a journalist.
Runaway Honeymoon features characters you will have read
about and enjoyed in Ruth Jean Dale's earlier novel,
Runaway Wedding.

Books by Ruth Jean Dale

Runaway
Honeymoon
Ruth Jean Dale

Harlequin Books

TORONTO • NEW YORK • LONDON
AMSTERDAM • PARIS • SYDNEY • HAMBURG
STOCKHOLM • ATHENS • TOKYO • MILAN
MADRID • WARSAW • BUDAPEST • AUCKLAND

You know how some folks "knew you when"
but like you anyway?
This book's for Donna,
who knew me *before* when!

ISBN 0-373-03441-5

RUNAWAY HONEYMOON

First North American Publication 1997.

CHAPTER ONE

JENNY Wolf shoved frantically at the tail of her old-fashioned white shirtwaist, trying to force it inside the waistband of her ankle-length skirt. She couldn't believe it—late for work on this of all days. She'd like to blame that darned alarm clock, for she rather vaguely remembered tapping the snooze button this morning. At least, that's what she'd intended to do. Apparently she'd simply turned off the alarm.

Straightening her skirt, she reached around to button it. "J.C.," she called, smoothing the navy blue fabric over her hips before hurrying to her makeup table. "We've got to hurry!"

"I am, Mom." The five-year-old's voice came faintly from the hallway. "But I can't find my Power Punchers T-shirt."

"Then wear another one." Jenny grabbed a brush and leaned sideways to drag the bristles through waist-length black hair. Dropping the brush, she scooped up the thick straight swatch and twisted it into a chignon atop her head.

J.C. appeared in her doorway, wearing color-ful knee-length shorts and nothing else. Tousled hair as dark as her own fell over his forehead. His mouth, usually curved in a smile, turned down at the corners. J.C. didn't like being rushed. He preferred to dawdle through life, stopping to smell the flowers...and study the

5

bugs . . . and the rocks. "Hurry" was not a word he enjoyed hearing—ever.

Jenny groaned. "Honey, we're *late*! We've just *got* to get a move on."

"We're always late," the boy declared.

"Not always. Once in a while—okay, frequently. But not today. Today is special." She jabbed hairpins into the cushion of hair, hoping they'd anchor firmly enough to hold.

"Why?"

"Oh, J.C.! Can't you take my word for it just this once?"

"I guess." He hesitated, his amber-brown eyes clear and curious. "But why?"

She knew from past experience that her inquisitive, intelligent son wouldn't give up until he got answers, however vague. "I told you last night," she reminded him. Cautiously she removed her hands from the mass of hair, which promptly proved too much for the pins and tumbled down around her shoulders. With a sigh, she reached for a coated rubber band. That's what she got for trying to rush, she supposed.

"Why." She leaned over to brush the hair over her head again before gathering it loosely into one hand for banding. "Because the hotel's been sold and the new owner's coming in today to meet everyone."

"Oh, yeah." A slight hesitation and then he added, "Don't the new owner—"

"Doesn't, honey." She sat up and began rearranging the dark mass of hair into a pouf. "*Doesn't* the new owner—?"

"Like you?" he finished.

"He'll like me more if I'm not late to work. Mr. Grover is used to me, but I'm afraid being late on his first day won't make a good impression on my new boss." She added in a muttered aside, "Although with any luck, he'll never find out."

She stuck in a final hairpin and gave her head a tentative shake. This time the bun stayed put, so she reached for her makeup case, hands trembling with tension. "J.C., please—"

"I'm goin'." Shoulders drooping to indicate his displeasure, he added, "But if I had a daddy, he wouldn't make me hurry." Turning, he shuffled back down the hall.

Jenny's stomach clenched painfully but she forced herself to open an eye shadow compact and go to work. She worked automatically, for her son's parting shot, however innocently uttered, had hit its target with unerring accuracy.

J.C. was both the joy and the trial of her life. She supposed they must be closer than most mothers and sons, since it was only the two of them and always had been. A father had never been part of his experience, and she had hoped against hope that what he'd never known, he'd never miss.

But as he grew older, she'd come to realize how futile that hope was. Now at the tender age of five, he was a veritable fount of questions and opinions—and many of those questions and opinions centered around the father he didn't even seem sure he'd had.

His mother had tried so very hard to give him a good life, to love and nurture him and be all things to him. But one thing she could not be, could never give him, was his father. Someday, she knew she'd have to tell J.C. the truth. But she rationalized that for his own sake, he must be old enough to handle it when she did.

She finished applying a subtle pink lipstick and recapped the tube, wondering when *she* would be old enough to handle it. "J.C.," she called, "I'm going to fix you a breakfast sandwich to eat on the way to the sitter's. I'm sorry, sweetheart, but we really have to get going."

Grabbing her high-button shoes, she lifted her long skirt and sprinted through the small cottage to the kitchen, making a point of ignoring the clock on the living room wall.

She knew she was late but she'd just as soon not know *how* late.

With J.C. fed, dressed and dropped off at the baby-sitter's, Jenny aimed her little four-wheel-drive vehicle down the side of the hill toward the Miner's Repose Hotel in the heart of Cripple Creek, Colorado. Trying not to drive too fast over rutted and unpaved streets, she took a deep breath and forced herself to look up to the distant peaks of the Sangre de Cristo Mountains toward the west, in an attempt to calm herself.

She and her brother, Jared, eight years older than her own twenty-six, had been born and raised in these Colorado mountains. They shared an almost mystical connection not only to the mountains but to the forests and streams of their native land. Perhaps it was the heritage of Indian blood—their great-grandfather had been a member of the Ute tribe—or perhaps it was their upbringing. Whatever it was, the Colorado wilderness held great power over them, both to soothe and to renew.

Feeling calmer, Jenny turned her thoughts forward. Yes, she was late, but she'd make up the time. If she was lucky, the new owner wouldn't even have to know—

A donkey trotted out of an alley, directly into the path of her car. She stepped on the brake and waited patiently for the little animal to move on, despite her need for haste. Any member of Cripple Creek's beloved donkey herd always had the right of way. Descended from donkeys brought here by miners during the great 1890's gold rush to transport gold ore, the furry critters were allowed—or more accurately, encouraged—to roam city streets from May to October, for the delight of tourists. Then the donkeys were rounded up and taken to winter pasture.

With Cripple Creek's Two-Mile-High Club to care for them, tourists and local residents to fuss over them, the donkeys had it made. They'd even had their own special festival every June since 1931—Donkey Derby Days, celebrated with much ado just last month.

The Miner's Repose was among local businesses fielding teams of five for the donkey race ever year. Jenny and four of her co-workers had come in second last month in what was billed as the Kentucky Derby of donkey-dom.

J.C. and every other child who saw the donkeys adored them, which was enough for Jenny. But she had to admit, by the time the little fellow in front of her decided to move on, she was about ready to climb out of her vehicle and offer encouragement.

The Miner's Repose Hotel first opened its doors on Myers Avenue in Cripple Creek in 1897, one year following the disastrous fires which wiped out nearly every building in the gold mining boomtown. That event, although horrifying, was not too surprising, considering the popularity at that time of the flimsy wood-framed buildings and canvas tents which had been so hastily thrown up to accommodate the miners. Six people died in the fires, and another five thousand left homeless until Cripple Creek could rebuild—with brick.

Jenny loved the stories of those rowdy early days. When she'd obtained a job as desk clerk at the Miner's Repose four years ago, she'd been presented with a ready-made excuse to delve even more deeply into local history. This she'd done with such thoroughness that she gradually became the hotel's resident expert, called upon to answer questions posed by the multitude of tourists passing through, especially after small-stakes gambling came to town in the fall of 1991.

Jenny also loved her job, which required, or more accurately *allowed*, her to dress in turn-of-the-century clothing and comport herself like a lady of that bygone era. That is, she liked everything except the shoes she felt obliged to wear, which is why they rested on the bucket seat beside her when she pulled into the parking lot behind the hotel. In actual fact, Jenny preferred going barefoot; she didn't like wearing *any* shoes.

The town was already alive with tourists, she noted, skipping across the lot between vehicles and entering the back door. Although the permanent population of Cripple Creek was only about twelve-hundred people, visitors poured in by the thousands each day during the summer months.

Jenny, for one, welcomed them with open arms. Without the tourists, the Miner's Repose would never have been renovated and reopened, even on its current diminished scale. With the hotel's historic past, it deserved better than the neglect which had nearly led to its final destruction.

"Jenny!"

Hearing her name, Jenny stopped short and turned. Nona Morris, Mr. Grover's secretary, motioned frantically from a doorway. Quickly Jenny hurried to the woman's side, raising her brows in a question.

Nona looked around quickly, causing the pencil thrust into her gray bun to quiver. Her brown eyes looked almost owlish above the granny glasses. "You're late," she whispered.

This was hardly news. "I'm sorry," Jenny said contritely. "I got to playing with J.C. last night and we were having such a good time—and then after he finally went to sleep I had to do laundry and iron and—"

"No time for that!" Nona exclaimed. "Mr. Grover's showing the new owner around and I'm afraid they know you're late."

"Rats!" Jenny bit her lip. "I was hoping I could kind of...you know, sneak in."

"Too late for that, I'm afraid. I'd recommend you get yourself out there behind that counter and act like nothing's happened. Maybe the new guy will forget. If he does, you know Mr. Grover won't make an issue of it. He says that even when you're late, he gets more work out of you than any three employees around here—and he gets it with a smile. The new owner, though—" She shook her head doubtfully.

Jenny's heart sank. "What's he like, Nona?"

The woman shrugged plump shoulders. "I haven't got the foggiest. But if you ask me, he's too good-looking to be a worthwhile human being."

"Nona!" Jenny was shocked at the woman's attitude.

"Well," Nona said defensively, "you haven't seen him. He's a real stud-muffin—tall, dark and handsome, as we used to say in my day. It seems to me people that good-looking always try to get by on it, if you know what I mean."

"I hope you're wrong," Jenny said, "for all our sakes."

"Time will tell." Nona patted the younger woman on the arm. "Now you get yourself in there and get busy. We don't want our new owner to get the wrong idea."

Jenny certainly didn't. With a grateful glance, she hurried down the hall and entered the lobby through the back. Racing across the royal blue carpeting with bare feet flying, she tossed her shoes onto a shelf behind the elaborately carved and curved registration desk.

At the other work station, Faith Stafford glanced up with a relieved smile before turning to the next customer. The lobby was full of people, some lining up to register but many wandering around to admire the historic photos and artifacts displayed on walls covered with gold-flocked wallpaper.

"Miss, if you could give me a little help here—"

Jenny smiled at the plump gentleman speaking so impatiently. "I'll be glad to," she said. "How may I be of service, sir?" By the time he left a few minutes later with key in hand, she had him laughing and joking with her. It was going to be another delightful day at the Miner's Repose. She only regretted that it had started without her.

She greeted the next customer with a smile, and the next—

Passing the large leather registration book back and forth between them, Faith and Jenny quickly and efficiently handled the crisis. Jenny began to relax a little, convinced that her personal crisis was also past. The new boss hadn't appeared yet, so in all likelihood he'd forgotten about the errant employee.

She hoped so, for she wanted to make a good impression on him. She liked her job but even more important, she needed it to support herself and her son—her brother Jared's offers of help to the contrary. Jared had made a ton of money in electronics before selling everything at the time of his marriage. He and his wife, Lark, had rees-

tablished the family's old Wolf Creek Ranch and
now lived there with their nine-month-old son—
named John Gray Wolf for his several-times-
great-grandfather. They raised horses and cows
and were happy as...Jenny smiled at the thought:
happy as larks.

Over the years since J.C.'s birth, Jenny had
accepted a limited amount of financial help from
her brother although he was constantly pushing
her to let him do more. Her independence was
important to her, and she thought he'd finally
come to understand that. Her pride recoiled at
the mere thought of handouts. Only in an
emergency, or for J.C.'s well-being, could she
swallow that pride.

But never easily. She was determined to take
care of herself and her child. With her income
from this job and a frugal life-style—

Sighing, she turned toward Faith, who also
wore the white-shirtwaist-and-dark-walking-skirt
costume which was uniform of the day for the
hotel's women employees. "Wow, that was quite
a rush. I'm really sorry I was—"

Faith's gaze skipped past Jenny and she let out
her breath in a soft gasp. Someone else wanting
to register, Jenny interpreted, turning with a
practiced smile—

—to find herself looking into a grown-up
version of her son's amber-brown eyes. She had
a quick impression of her boss, Mr. Grover,
standing beside the newcomer with an anxious
smile, and then all the air whooshed out of her
lungs. For a moment, she actually felt as if she
might faint.

Her new boss, the new owner of the Miner's Repose Hotel, was Cole Stadler, the father of her child.

For all Jenny knew, she might have actually passed out standing upright on her bare feet, for the next thing she knew Faith was sliding an arm around her waist and asking anxiously, "Are you all right? You look—"

"I'm fine," Jenny croaked, lying through her teeth and trying to work up the courage to risk another glance. It was J.C.'s question this morning that had brought Cole to mind; she was hallucinating. That's it, she was hallucinating. Straightening her shoulders, she forced herself to face the new owner of the Miner's Repose.

That man, heaven help her, was still Cole Stadler. A little flame leapt in the amber depths of his eyes, almost as if he were going through the same intense shock as she.

But when he spoke, it was ever so coolly. "Miss Lupo, I believe? Miss Geneva Lupo?"

His words were blows and she flinched before them. Fortunately, Mr. Grover intervened.

"Jennifer Wolf," the fatherly little gentleman corrected. "Miss Jennifer Wolf. Jenny's been with us since the hotel reopened four years ago. She's one of our best employees." He cleared his throat, then went on. "Jenny, this is the new owner of the hotel, Mr.—"

"She knows my name," Cole said smoothly. "At one time we were quite...well acquainted. Or so I thought."

Jenny knew she had to speak, but what could she say? Fortunately, Cole executed a swift about-face and walked into the manager's office, leaving her in abject terror.

This was awful—horrible! She'd worked so hard to put him out of her mind, and believed she'd succeeded. Now this had to happen, bringing everything back in a flash—

Jenny Wolf had been only twenty years old, an unsophisticated country girl with a rich fantasy life, when she and Sharon Goodman splurged on a singles cruise through the Panama Canal and into the Caribbean. The two had gone to high school together, then found work together as secretaries for the county department of roads. One day during lunch, they got to talking about their dream vacations and discovered that a luxury cruise was their shared fantasy. The next step was inevitable: two years of saving and planning and then, the big day finally arrived.

Flying out of Denver International Airport, they deplaned in Acapulco where they and other passengers heading for the cruise ship, *Inamorata II*, were met by small open-sided buses for the trip from the airport to one of the most beautiful harbors in the world.

The view from the bus hurtling down a jungle-green mountainside took Jenny's breath away. She could hardly believe she was really in Mexico; it felt like a dream. On an impulse, she'd turned to Sharon.

"I'm going to make the best of this vacation," she vowed. "It's a once-in-a-lifetime thing and nothing's going to hold me back. I'm going to see everything and try everything and have enough fun and adventure to last a lifetime.''

Their glances met, Jenny's blue eyes asking a question and Sharon's brown eyes offering confirmation.

''Nothing ventured, nothing gained,'' Sharon agreed, her voice trembling with excitement.

''Exactly. Gosh, Sharon, I feel so free, almost like a different person. This can't be happening to little Colorado mountain girl Jenny Wolf.''

''Then don't be Jenny Wolf,'' Sharon advised with a laugh. ''Be Jenny...Jenny Lobo! That's Spanish for wolf.''

''Lobo is too close to loco—and that's Spanish for crazy.''

Sharon grinned. ''Okay, how about—I've got it, lu-po?'' She said the word hesitantly, then with growing assurance. ''That's it, Lupo, Italian for wolf. My grandmother's Italian,'' she added confidentially. ''Jenny Lupo, that's you.''

''Jenny's too plain to go with Lupo,'' Jenny argued, getting into the spirit of the thing. ''How about Genevieve?''

''Too old-fashioned. How about Guinevere? No, that's too King Arthur-ish.'' They laughed together and then Sharon snapped her fingers. ''By George, I think I've got it! Geneva, Geneva Lupo, exotic woman of mystery. Live up to the name and this really *will* be the vacation of a lifetime.''

''*Geneva Lupo*.'' Jenny tried it out. *Could* she do it? Could she live up to such a name?

She might never have known, but for Sharon. Once through customs and up the gangplank onto the deck of the cruise ship, ever-friendly Sharon made a point of addressing Jenny as "Geneva," and introducing her that way to other passengers. They'd found their room on the Sweetheart Deck, tiny but with all the necessary amenities including a window, but didn't stay long. Rushing up to the main deck again, they'd joined the throngs of passengers leaning over the side to wave to those poor unfortunates being left behind on the shore.

But as the time for sailing neared, Jenny found herself feeling more and more overwhelmed by the crowd. Seeing Sharon in rapt conversation with an athletic-looking young man, she slipped away to stroll to the other side of the ship. Here, overlooking the bay, the crowd was much thinner. Jenny found a spot alone near the lifeboats and leaned against the glossy hardwood rail. The bay was literally filled with cruise ships, some larger and some smaller than her own, but all alluring.

She closed her eyes with a sigh, trying to convince herself that she was really here on day one of a ten-day adventure she could barely imagine.

"First cruise, I take it?"

At the softly spoken words, Jenny's eyes flew open and she saw that a man had magically appeared beside her. A man with amber-gold eyes and the nicest smile she'd ever seen, as a matter of fact. He wore white shorts and a pale blue knit shirt, and arms braced against the deck railing revealed a sinewy muscularity.

But it was his aura of confidence that really attracted her. Certainly, this wouldn't be *his* first cruise. She started to admit it was, indeed, *her* first, but something stopped her.

Would Geneva Lupo admit to such a thing? Jenny returned his smile. "What makes you think that?" she countered.

He shrugged broad shoulders. "I didn't, really. But it seemed a better ice-breaker than *a penny for your thoughts*." He straightened away from the rail. "I'm Cole Stadler," he said, his gaze catching and holding hers. "I have high hopes of seeing a lot of you on this cruise."

Slowly Jenny extended her hand. She found herself completely incapable of resisting the intimacy of his gaze. "I'm...Geneva Lupo," she said softly. "But my friends call me Jenny."

His strong fingers closed over her cold ones. "I have every expectation of being that, at least." He squeezed her hand lightly before releasing her to turn back to the fabulous view spread out before them. "I hope you don't mind if I join you."

For a moment she stared at him, then turned abruptly back to the rail herself. "Not at all," she said in the most negligent tone she could summon. But her heart pounded and she swallowed hard. Why would a handsome, sophisticated man like this one look twice at Jenny Wolf?

Perhaps a luxury cruise ship really did generate its own magic. Perhaps for a girl with the spirit to create a whole new identity for herself, anything was possible....

Including love, a broken heart and a baby, in that order. For a while, she'd dared to hope. He'd pressed a telephone number into her hand when they'd parted in Puerto Rico, but fate had been against her. Before she'd even stepped off the plane in Denver, she'd been shaking with chills. She'd ended up in the hospital for ten miserable days, then had been taken to her brother Jared's Denver home to recover.

She couldn't very well call Cole from Jared's house. If Jared ever found out about her and Cole, there was no telling what her hotheaded brother might do. So she'd bided her time, playing it safe until she could return to Cripple Creek and her secretarial job—only to discover she'd lost or misplaced his number.

In a panic, she'd taken apart everything that had been on the cruise with her. She finally found the number in the lining of her jacket, where it had apparently worked its way through a small hole in the seam. By then, six weeks had passed. Instead of reaching a person, a telephone answering machine picked up every time she called. It took another three weeks before she reached a real live person. When she did, what she heard broke her heart.

Before she'd recovered from that blow, she received another. She was pregnant....

That cruise had changed her life, all right, but she'd managed to come to terms with her past and find joy in the son who had completely redirected her future. She had never expected to hear that name again: *Geneva Lupo*.

She had to think—

But employees of the Miner's Repose clustered around her, their questions flying quick and fast. "You *know* the new boss? Why didn't you tell us, Jenny? What's he like? How did you meet him? What's he *really* like?"

Question after question, and she couldn't answer any of them.

Wouldn't, even if she could...

CHAPTER TWO

CRIPPLE CREEK!

Now Cole Stadler knew why the name of this little Colorado mining town way up in the Rocky Mountains had struck such a responsive chord the first time his father mentioned it.

Sitting behind the antique desk in his new office off the hotel lobby, he picked up a paperweight and turned it over and over in numb hands. The paperweight was a nugget of Cripple Creek gold encased in crystal, Clarence Grover had explained. The nugget had been found during renovations of the Miner's Repose Hotel.

Gritting his teeth, Cole replaced the paperweight on the shiny desktop. She was out there, just beyond that wall with the ancient photograph of an old miner and a donkey.

After all these years...

He'd met Geneva Lupo—check that, Jenny Wolf—six years ago on a cruise which began in Acapulco and proceeded to the Caribbean by way of the Panama Canal. He'd been twenty-six at the time, at a personal crossroads. He'd been looking for anonymity and space to decide what he wanted out of life: marriage to the girl next door and the comfortable, if often uncomfortably limiting life as a hotel magnate's son and heir; or a clean break in search of adventure and

high romance—romance in the sense of heroic
and adventurous deeds.

Time was running out. His marriage to Lynette
Davis, his childhood sweetheart, was mere weeks
away. The San Francisco church was booked, the
reception planned; his parents were delighted, her
parents were thrilled. The bride-to-be sailed serenely through the plans and parties, while the
bridegroom-to-be slipped closer and closer to the
point of outright rebellion.

It had been Lynette's idea for him to get away.
"Anywhere," she said, patting his hand with
perfectly manicured nails. "A spa, a dude ranch,
a beach—whatever appeals to you, darling. I'm
afraid if you don't get out of this three-ring
circus, you won't be *fit* to marry." She kissed
him lightly on the cheek before turning back to
her lists and samples. "I'd like to talk more but
the wedding consultant is waiting—"

At first, the idea had seemed ridiculous; just
walk away with so much to be done? But then
the best man had wrapped his Porsche around a
tree and ended up in the hospital, unable to take
advantage of a reservation on the *Inamorata II*.
When Cole visited the pitiful individual so encased in bandages that he more nearly resembled
an Egyptian mummy than a man, he'd been en-
trusted with the cancellation.

Was this fate at work? Solitude, ocean breezes
and the music of steel bands might be just what
Cole needed. Of course, Lynette wouldn't go for
it; she'd protect him from himself.

Only she hadn't. With her usual absent enthusiasm, she'd suggested that this might be just

the ticket. He should go and have a good time.
Her attitude further frayed his nerves. If that's
all she had to say on the subject, he was out of
there.

He was in a foul mood when he boarded the
cruise ship, and he made a point of distancing
himself from the crowd of pleasure-seekers. Even
so, he hadn't been aboard for ten minutes when
he spotted the beautiful girl standing alone near
the lifeboats on the bayside of the cruise ship.

There was something exotic about her, perhaps
helped along by the most glorious head of hair
he'd ever seen. Hair wasn't his thing; he'd never
much noticed a woman's hair before. But hers
was long—to her waist, at least—and as black as
night. Straight and shiny, it almost crackled with
vitality.

A light breeze stirred that glorious mass and
she wrapped an arm around her head to brush it
back. Even her arm was gracefully formed. From
his angle slightly behind and to one side of her,
he couldn't see her face but was instantly aware
of the rise of her breast, the slenderness of her
waist above her hips. Beneath the hem of her
flowered skirt, her honey-brown calves curved
down into slim, well-formed ankles.

He'd said something inane—he didn't remember what. She'd turned toward him, a
question on her face, and her beauty almost took
his breath away. Her eyes were blue, sapphire
blue, slightly almond-shaped in a face dis-
tinguished by sculpted cheekbones and a mouth
as full and ripe as summer strawberries. Later,
he would realize that he fell in love with her

before he ever heard her voice. At the time he'd called it infatuation, and rationalized that a simple and harmless flirtation was all he'd had in mind.

He'd barely been able to drag himself away from Geneva to allow them both time to unpack. They'd met on deck at sunset for drinks—lemonade for her, which he found curiously endearing. Standing side-by-side, she'd told him a story about the ghosts of unrequited lovers wandering the corridors of an old, tumble-down hotel in... *Cripple Creek*.

He hadn't even known where Cripple Creek was. When she told him it was in the Colorado mountains, he'd asked if that was where she came from.

"I'm a citizen of the world," she said lightly, playing with a thick strand of that incredible hair. "Someone told me the story. Sometimes I live in Monterey, which has its own ghosts—"

"California? Small world. I'm from San Francisco."

"Or San Antonio, Texas," she said quickly. "The Alamo is full of ghosts. Of course, Boston's a favorite of mine—"

He knew she wasn't exactly lying but she wasn't necessarily telling the truth, either. Somehow that seemed all right in these unreal surroundings, where nothing was important except food and drink and fun. She intrigued him more than any woman he'd ever met, and he supposed that was just part of the holiday package. Certainly, he wouldn't let things go too far between them—

Dinner that first night, before Cole had time to arrange for them to share the same table, was agony. She'd been assigned a seat next to some idiot in nautical whites who looked like a real motor-mouth, from Cole's admittedly poor vantage point. But afterward, she was all his.

They took in a lounge show, drifted through the casino without so much as putting a quarter in a slot machine, and ended up at the midnight buffet beside the pool on the top deck. Warm tropical breezes gently stirred her hair, and he couldn't resist reaching out to smooth the midnight-dark strands away from her face. She didn't pull away, simply gave him a look so quizzical that he surrendered to temptation without even token resistance.

When he drew her into his arms, she came without hesitation. His mouth brushed hers in a kiss more tentative than any he'd ever bestowed. This was moving too fast, and if he knew it so must she. Yet she simply slid her arms around his neck and let her mouth go soft and yearning beneath his own.

When at last he broke off the kiss, she stepped away with a breathless little laugh that tore at his restraint. Later while they feasted on lobster and strawberries, she'd told him another whimsically romantic story... and then another and another, some more outrageous than her tale of ghosts and unrequited love.

He didn't care. He was falling under her spell— and he didn't even know how old she was, or if she had a family, or even if she was married. He wanted to ask, but then she might pose the same questions and he wasn't ready to provide answers.

By the fourth day, they were lovers and all else was mere detail. He'd had a difficult moment, then, believing—after it was too late to do anything about it—that she was a virgin. She'd assured him that was not the case. It had simply been a long time for her, she said, nothing to be concerned about.

And then she'd wrapped her arms about him and kissed him and he *wasn't* concerned, not anymore.

She was traveling with a friend who, fortunately or not, had her own agenda. That meant Jenny could give Cole all her time and attention. They did everything together, from exercise classes first thing in the morning to midnight buffets. They'd wander hand-in-hand to Cole's suite with its own balcony out over the sea, much larger and more luxurious than her own shared room. There they made love, often watching the sun come up over the water while they lay in each other's arms.

By the eighth day, Cole knew he wanted to spend the rest of his life with her. He tried to call ship-to-shore to tell Lynette so, but was unable to reach her.

On the tenth day, the cruise ship reached Puerto Rico and the dream threatened to come apart at the seams. In the crush of disembarking passengers, he'd fought to find her—and she to find him. When she was finally in his arms, he'd slipped a diamond ring on her finger, a ring he'd bought following a quick telephone call to a jeweler in St. Thomas.

"But—" Frowning, she'd looked up at him with an expression painful in its vulnerability. "What *is* this?"

"I want to call it an engagement ring but I can't quite yet," he'd said in all honesty. "Let's call it a friendship ring. There are things I have to do first...."

She nodded, moving the ring around and around on her finger and staring down at the enormous, glittering stone as if she couldn't believe it was really there. "I understand," she whispered. She looked up at him again, licking her lips. "I... never expected this to happen."

"You mean you and me? Neither did I." He gave her a quick, hard kiss on the lips. "I know you've got to catch one of the early buses to the airport so I can't keep you as much as I want to." He thrust a slip of paper at her. "Call me here," he commanded. "It's my family home, where you can always reach me. Where can I reach you?"

"You can't," she said quickly. "I'll contact you one week from today, I promise."

He hesitated, believing in her with all his heart but unwilling to let her go this way. But if she had secrets, things she had to take care of, didn't he, also?

He'd never seen or heard from her again.

She had never intended to keep her promises. She'd simply taken his expensive ring and disappeared without a trace.

But Cole had never forgotten—or forgiven. Through the intervening years, he'd promised himself that if he ever found Geneva Lupo again, she'd have a lot to answer for—a hell of a lot.

Sitting in his office in the Miner's Repose Hotel, he remembered asking his father in all innocence, "Why are you telling me about some rundown little hotel in Cripple Creek, Colorado?"

Because, his father had replied, he'd decided to acquire the property for World Heritage Hotels, the Stadler family enterprise that specialized in renovating and running old hotels all over the world.

"The potential is there," John Stadler had mused. "I know you're looking for a project of your own, a chance to show what you can do. This might be just the ticket." He'd tossed a fat manila folder onto the conference table. "I'm not trying to force you into anything, son, but if you're interested..."

Cole was more than interested; in fact, he'd felt almost drawn to the project.

Now he knew why.

It seemed as if the morning would never end. Jenny, who was slated for late lunch, thought one o'clock would never roll around.

Everyone was giving her the fish eye. When it had become clear that she wouldn't, or couldn't, answer any questions about the new boss, her fellow workers had backed off—verbally, anyway. The questions were still there in the looks they gave her.

Everything was in order at the front desk, all entered and tabulated and ready for the most discerning inspection. Faith had even come back a few minutes early from her own lunch. Maybe—

The ornate front door swung open and a pretty woman with curly red-blond hair and a baby-pack on her shoulders entered. When she saw Jenny, she smiled and waved.

Jenny smiled back. Her sister-in-law, Lark, was one of her best friends and favorite people. And naturally, she also had a soft spot in her heart for her nephew, nine-month-old John Gray Wolf.

Lark reached the registration desk and leaned her elbows on the counter. "Hi, sweetie," she said. "Jared's off at the feed store and then he's got to get a tire fixed so Gray and I thought if you hadn't had lunch yet—"

She stopped short, her gaze lifting and her hazel eyes going wide.

Somehow Jenny knew; she just knew he was behind her, even before she felt his hand on her elbow or heard his voice.

"Miss Wolf has a prior engagement," Cole said, and there was no room for argument in his tone. "If you'll excuse us—"

"But—" Jenny tried to shrug out of his iron grip without creating a scene, which of course, he must be counting on. He whisked her around the counter and out the door before she could get herself set to resist.

On the sidewalk out front, she finally managed to shake free. "What do you think you're doing?" she demanded. "That's my sister-in-law in there. You can't just—just *impose* yourself on me this way."

"Touching you is imposing?" His laugh sounded cynical. "You didn't always call it that."

"Oh, Cole..." She felt completely helpless, just as she had on the cruise ship. But before, her love had made her vulnerable. Now she supposed it was her guilt.

He took her arm again and she steeled herself not to react, then felt a shiver ripple through her anyway.

"Come to lunch, Jenny," he ordered, "unless you want to cause a scene."

A scene with the father of her child? She would avoid that at all costs. Not even Jared and Lark knew the identity of J.C.'s father—didn't even know the boy was named *Cole* for that father; they thought J.C.'s middle name was Charles.

For his part, that father had no idea Jenny even *had* a child. Looking up into that handsome face, she realized that Cole had far more with which to coerce her to do his bidding than even he could imagine. Her stomach plummeted at that knowledge.

"All right." She gave in with a sigh. "But can't we have lunch right here in our own dining room?" She frowned. "Why are you shaking your head?"

"I don't want to be interrupted and we surely would be in there. We'll go someplace else."

"Where?" Still suspicious, she planted her high-button shoes on the sidewalk and refused to move.

Fire leapt into his amber eyes. "Where?" he echoed softly. "*Any damned place I say*, Miss Wolf." And grabbing her hand, he hauled her down the sidewalk toward Bennett Avenue as fast as she could go.

Cole closed his menu. "I'll have a buffalo burger and a glass of ice tea," he told the waitress. He glanced at Jenny. "How about you?"

"I've had buffalo burgers," she said.

"Have you had escargot?"

She felt the blush climb up her throat and across her cheeks. He would have to bring up her incredulous reaction when she'd been served snails on board the *Inamorata*—not exactly what he might have expected from a sophisticate. "I've had escargot as often as I care to," she countered grimly.

"Good," the waitress put in tartly, "because we're all out of that."

Biting her lip, Jenny quickly studied her menu. Who was she kidding? She wouldn't be able to eat with Cole sitting across from her in the booth. She glanced at the patient waitress, who might not be so much patient as interested in the new boss of the Miner's Repose. "I'll just have a salad, Rosie," Jenny decided. "Ranch dressing on the side, please, and ice tea."

"You got it, Jenny." The waitress turned away, scribbling on her pad as she went. "I'll bring them teas right away."

Now what? Jenny wondered, twisting her hands into a knot in her lap. He was staring at her as if he hated her, when he was the one who—

"So what have you been up to in the last five or six years?" he asked suddenly, his tone caustic. "Been on any good cruises?"

"No, I haven't been on any cruises, good or otherwise. After what happened the last time, you don't think I'd—" She stopped, appalled. He wouldn't have the first idea what she was talking about. "I . . . haven't had time," she continued lamely. "I'm a working girl, after all."

"Nice work if you can get it." His gaze pinned her to her seat.

"W-what's that supposed to mean?" He had her completely off balance and struggling to keep up with his conversational shifts. How had she once thought him the easiest person in the world to be with?

He traced a scratch in the booth top with a well-manicured thumbnail. "Somebody was late to work this morning. I didn't hear any names tossed about but the process of elimination leads me to conclude it was you."

She hung her head guiltily, well aware that she couldn't point out she'd have made it if J.C. hadn't dawdled so. "I'll try not to let it happen again," she murmured.

"Try *hard*. Clarence Grover grudgingly admitted that you're late on an average of three days a week. Of course, he also insists you're a model employee once you get there, the best he's got." He waited until Rosie had served their drinks and departed before continuing. "Perhaps that lax attitude is the reason he couldn't make a go of the Miner's Repose. The hotel has everything going for it and should be a great success."

"That's not the reason at all," Jenny denied. "His attitude isn't lax, it's—it's considerate. He takes extenuating circumstances into account—"

"What extenuating circumstances?" Cole asked quickly.

That hard amber gaze pummeled her. She bit her lip, knowing she couldn't tell him that Mr. Grover understood how difficult it was for a single mother to hold down a full-time job.

He pressed for an answer. "I'm waiting. What extenuating circumstances, besides the usual—late hours and high living?"

He was pushing too hard, making her angry. She lifted her chin and glared at him. "Look, *Mr.* Stadler, you can fire me but you can't give me the third degree. If that's why you dragged me here, you've wasted your time."

"I doubt it. I expect you got my message, Miss Lupo. Three strikes and you're out. Is that clear?"

"Quite clear." Her jaw was beginning to ache, it was set so stiff.

"And you've already got one strike."

Before Jenny could tell him what to do with the other two, Rosie plunked down the salad and the burger. "Dressing on the side." She placed a small bowl before Jenny. "You folks need anything else?"

"Not at the moment." Cole favored her with a brilliant smile and Jenny looked away. "Thanks, Rosie."

"Anytime, Mr. Stadler." The waitress grinned. "And welcome to Cripple Creek. Your kind is always an asset to our fair city, I do declare." Giving him a broad wink, she sashayed away.

Cole laughed and the sound tore at Jenny's nerves. That was the laugh she remembered, an indulgent and approving sound that sent a warm shiver down her spine. Heaven help her, he was a charmer, at least when it suited his purpose.

While he devoured his buffalo burger, Jenny poked at her salad and pretended to eat. She hadn't even begun to come to terms with his sudden appearance and knew she wouldn't be able to start sorting out her feelings until she had some time alone. She'd have to work a half hour late tonight to make up for her tardiness this morning, but fortunately J.C.'s sitter had no problem with erratic hours.

Oh, J.C.! What would this mean to him?

Cole finished his burger, wiped his mouth and fingers with the paper napkin and dropped it beside his plate. He glanced at her barely touched salad with condemnation. "Do you plan to eat that or just play with it?"

She dropped her fork and glared at him. "May I be excused? I'd like to go back to work now."

"You may not. I brought you here—"

"*Dragged* me here."

"—for a purpose."

"Yes, and I know what it is—to humiliate me. You've already done that, so if you have no further objection—"

"I'll have no objection after you answer one question."

She sucked in a deep breath and pressed her lips together, waiting.

"*Why didn't you call when you said you would*?"

There it was, right out in the open; no more pussyfooting around, no more dodging the real issue. Perhaps she should be grateful that he'd laid his complaint on the table.

Still, she stammered out her reply. "Well, I was sick. I got off the plane and Jared took me—"

"Jared?" Anger flashed in his eyes.

"My brother. That was his wife you insulted back at the hotel."

"I see. Please go on. You were saying you had a cold—"

"I had some awful tropical germ! Jared took me straight from the airport to the hospital and I was flat on my back for ten days."

"And then you got well, because here you are."

"*Then* I went to my brother's house for two more weeks."

"This brother doesn't have a telephone?"

"Of course he does, but I didn't want your number on his telephone bill because he'd have asked a lot of questions I wasn't prepared to answer."

"I see." He didn't look as if he did; his expression was just as hard as it had been since they'd arrived at the restaurant. "And after that?"

She bit her lip. "I...lost your number."

He gripped the edge of the table so tightly that the dishes jumped. "Give me a break," he said softly. "You lost the—?"

"Well, I did. But then I—"

"Give it up, Jenny."

"You asked!"

"Okay, I take back the question. I don't need to hear any more. All you're offering are excuses and pretty lame ones at that. You never intended to call. You were leading me on—"

"I never did! I meant everything I said, everything I did—"

"If that were true, you wouldn't have given up efforts to reach me so easily. Why are you feeding me this line of—"

"Because I know!" Anguish spilled over into her voice. "I finally found that number you gave me. It had slipped through a tiny hole in a pocket seam of my jacket. I practically had to take the jacket apart to find it."

"Oh, really." He sounded bored but he didn't look it; he looked furious.

"Yes, really."

"Funny, I don't recall any messages from you, or even hearing you'd telephoned."

For a very long, very tense moment she stared at him. Then she said, "You mean your *wife* didn't mention it?"

Before he could respond, she leapt from the booth and hurried out of the restaurant.

* * *

He caught up with her before she could reach the sanctuary of her post of duty, if indeed it could have offered safety. Grabbing her arm, he hauled her through the lobby and straight into his office, leaving other employees gaping after them. It was humiliating, but he gave her no time to think about that.

Once the ornate door closed behind them, he swung her around to face him. "Explain," he ordered flatly.

"What is there to explain? When I finally got through, to the number you gave me, a woman answered. When I asked for you, she said I could give her the message, since she was your wife." She bit her lip and looked away. "I didn't believe her—I didn't want to believe her. So I said, 'You mean you're married to *Cole Stadler*?' And she laughed and said that was right, you'd been married for almost a month."

Finally she forced herself to look up into his face. "It's true, isn't it? You went home from our—the cruise and married another woman."

His expression didn't soften. "That's right— but only after it became glaringly apparent that Miss Geneva Lupo, a.k.a. Jenny Wolf, was a two-timing little bitch." His condemning gaze raked her. "I hope you got a good price for that diamond, by the way. It cost a bundle, even in St. Thomas."

"Diamond? But I thought—" She frowned. "Didn't you buy it at the ship gift shop? They had a lot of pretty rings there, zircons and imitations—"

"Don't tell me some slick jeweler stiffed you on the sale." He didn't look amused by the prospect.

She rubbed her arms where his fingers had bitten into her flesh. "No, of course not. I didn't sell it. I'd never do that."

"Then where is it? You're not wearing it."

"Why it's—" She stopped short. It was in a tiny velvet bag at the bottom of her jewelry case, to be passed on to J.C. when he was grown. It was intended to be the only remembrance his mother could give him of his father.

But she dared not so much as mention J.C.'s name. Oh, if only she could have time to think—

"Yeah," Cole said, "that's what I thought. No reason you shouldn't sell it. It was a gift, after all, with negligible sentimental value."

"It's not what you think," Jenny said miserably, then remembered that she was the injured party here and lifted her chin. "At least I didn't rush home and marry someone else. What did you do, elope?"

"I was married in an enormous church wedding with all the trimmings."

"But how—?"

"I was engaged when I went on that cruise for the express purpose of figuring out whether or not I wanted to go through with it. When I told you I had business to take care of before I could call that diamond an engagement ring, that's the business I meant—breaking it off with Lynette."

"I...don't believe you." She *dared not* believe him.

"I don't give a—" He stopped, sucked in a deep breath and continued calmly. "When you failed to call, it didn't seem to matter much what I did. Since it meant so much to her, and to both sets of parents..." He shrugged as if he'd satisfactorily explained everything.

Only he hadn't, especially when his eyes narrowed and he took a step toward Jenny. How could he look at her as if he had some insane idea of picking up where they'd left off six years ago, when he'd just admitted he had a wife sitting at home in San Francisco?

CHAPTER THREE

JENNY hardly knew how she was going to get through the rest of the day. Everywhere she looked, she saw Cole Stadler watching her...always watching her. She hoped she was the only person who recognized that assessing expression in his tawny eyes.

As usual, she shared her afternoon break in the tiny employee lounge with Nona Morris. The grandmotherly woman had been Mr. Grover's secretary since the Miner's Repose opened and now Nona was about to fulfill the same function for the new owner.

"But I haven't agreed to a thing yet," Nona declared, blowing on her coffee to cool it. "He's been nice enough so far, but I'm reserving judgment. Men that good-looking aren't to be trusted." She slanted a measured glance in Jenny's direction. "So they tell me you already know Mr. Stadler."

Jenny clenched icy fingers into a knot in her lap. "We...met a few years ago."

"Uh-huh." Nona's brown eyes were shrewd. "It's all over the hotel that he took you to lunch." She looked suddenly sympathetic. "Did he chew you out for being late this morning?"

Jenny nodded; well, he *had*.

"I figured as much," Nona said grimly. "That's just the sort of thing that worries me.

Doesn't he know how hard it is for a young mother—"

"Oh, please, you didn't say anything to him about J.C.!"

Nona frowned. "Well, no, but maybe I should."

"Don't! Promise me you won't say a word— or let any of the others say anything, either." Jenny leaned forward earnestly. "I should be judged on the job I do here, just like the rest of you, not on my...my family situation. Mr. Grover was so n-nice to me that maybe I *did* take advantage of his good nature."

"Hogwash! You've never taken advantage of anyone in your life, Jennifer Wolf."

"Thanks for your vote of confidence." Jenny looked at her companion with gratitude. "Still, rules are made for everybody. I'm going to try my darnedest to be on time from here on out."

Nona sighed. "Maybe that'd be a good idea, considering we're none of us too sure what we're up against," she agreed. Cocking her head, she added thoughtfully, "Except maybe you..."

Jenny returned to work and couldn't get Cole out of her mind. It didn't help that every time she turned around, she saw him.

His enigmatic expression was driving her crazy. What did he expect from her? Trying to figure that out almost drove her crazy.

When he summoned her into his office minutes before quitting time, she was almost relieved to confront him. She stood before his big wooden desk and waited, trying to prepare herself for anything but expecting only one thing: to be fired.

He leaned back in the old-fashioned office chair, his gaze on her steady and filled with speculation. "Grover tells me you're his resident expert on local history," he said. "On the ship—"

She caught her breath sharply, her eyes opening wider. "Do we have to talk about that?" Oh, dear, she shouldn't sound so pleading.

"Does it make you uncomfortable?"

Nobody knew how much! She shook her head. "Not at all. It just seems to me we'd be better off letting bygones be b-bygones."

For a moment he met her gaze, his own narrow and thoughtful. "If you can do that—well, never mind. I only brought up the ship because that's where you told me the stories."

"What stories?"

"About ghosts in Cripple Creek. All day long I've been trying to remember."

Jenny felt both relieved and disconcerted. "Goodness, I hardly remember myself."

"I suppose it must have meant more to me." His golden eyes condemned her. "I seem to remember one about a ghost named . . . Kitty?"

She nodded, in her element again. "The Palace Hotel over on Bennett Avenue has a ghost believed to be that of a woman named Kitty Chambers who died there about 1908. Her specialty is lighting candles—or used to be. She hasn't been seen or heard from much since gambling brought in so many new people a few years back."

He shook his head. "That's not the one I was thinking about." He picked up a pencil and turned it between long, capable fingers. "What— or perhaps I should say, *who* else?"

"There's George over at the Imperial."

"A ghost named George?"

The way he said it, with a lift of his eyebrows and a humorous tilt to his lips, reminded her of the Cole Stadler she'd fallen in lov— She swallowed hard. "They say George's wife killed him by hitting him over the head with a skillet. Since they lived at the Imperial Hotel, that's still his favorite haunt, so to speak."

Again, Cole shook his head. "That's not the one, either. The one I'm thinking of is a much more romantic story, something to do with a...a honeymoon? Or maybe it was a bridal suite. Something like that, anyway."

Jenny gasped, realizing he'd caught her neatly in a trap of her own making. She remembered now; she'd told him about the ghost at the Miner's Repose. The hotel hadn't even reopened at the time, and was nothing more than a shattered shell of its former glorious self. But the ghost was one of the best known in Cripple Creek, probably in all of Colorado.

Cole smiled. "Ah," he said softly. "I see you remember."

Jenny nodded. "Of course. Our ghost—"

"*Our* ghost?"

"Your ghost, then. I suppose you acquired him along with everything else when you bought the Miner's Repose. Anyway, there used to be a honeymoon suite on the fourth floor here but it wasn't refurbished before the hotel was re-opened. Mr. Grover kept meaning to—''

"The ghost story, Jenny.''

"Of course, the ghost story.'' She lifted her gaze until she found herself staring at the flowered wallpaper border just below the high ceiling. It was easier than looking at Cole Stadler.

"Well," she began, "they say that a beautiful young girl and a handsome young man were to be married shortly after the Miner's Repose first opened in 1899. He was a miner, of course, one of many men trying to court her—unsuccessfully, until he made what everyone thought was a big gold strike.''

"I sense tragedy,'' Cole said with raised eyebrows.

"I know few if any ghost stories that resulted from happily-ever-afters,'' she said tartly. "As the story goes, while the young couple exchanged their vows, they received bad news—the mine was a bust. Still, he was happy because he loved her. On the spot, he vowed to find another fortune for her.''

"Poor shmuck.''

Jenny's cheeks flushed. "Do you want to hear this or don't you?''

"I do, I do.''

"The young wife seemed distracted, but she told her husband to go ahead to the bridal suite and wait for her there, that she'd join him shortly.'' Jenny bit her lip, returning her gaze resolutely to the narrow strip of flowered paper near the ceiling. "She never came.''

"At this point in the original telling," Cole inserted, "I seem to remember putting my arms around you and kissing you and telling you there was no need to go on. I knew what happened next. She probably caught the first train to Denver while her discarded mate hanged himself from the chandelier or some such."

She met his cynical gaze at last. "Not exactly. She was run down in the street by a horse and carriage and died without telling anyone where she was going or what she planned to do. Her husband was inconsolable, and he *did* hang himself. His ghost has wandered the halls of the Miner's Repose ever since, but most of the sightings have been in or near the bridal suite. The story goes that his spirit won't be free until a truly happy couple honeymoons there, which seems unlikely to happen since strange things keep causing the suite to remain closed."

"Strange how?"

She shrugged. "Fires, water damage, lightning strikes, electrical problems—you name it. There are those who think the heart-broken bridegroom is behind it all."

"Have you ever seen him?"

"No."

"I have." He wasn't smiling when he said it. "But then, I've moved into his suite."

She couldn't have been more shocked. "You're *living* in the bridal suite?"

"Why not? Since it isn't in shape for guests, it seemed logical enough."

"Good heavens," she said faintly. "And you saw him?"

"I saw someone, a man in old-fashioned clothing who said his name was—"

"He *spoke* to you?"

He nodded. "He said his name was Able, but nobody could tell me afterward who he might be or what he was doing in my private quarters." He smiled suddenly, that quick, warm smile she'd once loved so. "Or maybe it was a dream. Who knows? The line between dreams and reality is often blurred."

"Yes, well..." She shifted uneasily, wondering if he were talking about the past or the present. "If there's nothing else—"

"There is, but it'll have to wait." He rose with casual grace. "I'm looking forward to hearing more about my new community."

Her heart sank. Surely he didn't intend to force his company upon her in the name of history.

He went on. "But I'm keeping you. It's a few minutes past your quitting time."

"I'll be working a half hour late, to make up for my tardy arrival this morning. I guess this is as good a time as any to apologize for that."

"Three strikes," he reminded her softly, "and you're out."

"You made that very clear at lunch." She lifted her chin. "If that's all...?"

"For the moment, Miss Lupo. For the moment."

Walking out of his office, she could feel his gaze sharp as a knife between her shoulder blades.

* * *

When Jenny and J.C. arrived at their small home on the hillside above Cripple Creek, they found Jared, Lark and baby Gray waiting for them. Lark jumped out of the Jeep Cherokee at the sight of them, a stack of pizza boxes in her hands, while Jared followed with the baby.

Lark smiled broadly. "You're late," she said, watching her sister-in-law and nephew climb out of Jenny's little car. "We were beginning to wonder if we were going to have to eat these two huge pizzas all by ourselves."

"Cheese pizzas?" J.C. asked hopefully. He was going through a phase where he picked everything else off, even his immediate past favorite, pepperoni.

"One of them's cheese, just for you." Lark leaned down and gave him a kiss on the cheek. "How's my boy?"

"I'm good, Aunt Lark. I caught some bugs today—wanna see 'em?"

They moved together toward the house. Smiling, Jenny turned to greet her brother, holding out her arms for Gray. Jared deposited the baby in her embrace and she covered his chubby cheeks with kisses. "How's my angel?" she cooed. "Oh, Jared, he's growing like a weed!"

"He sure is." Her handsome, dark-haired brother smiled with evident pride. "How's it going with you, baby sister?"

"Never better." She led him toward the house, picking her way carefully across the yard since her feet were bare. She'd have to remember tomorrow that she'd left her high-buttoned shoes in the car.

Lark had already opened the cardboard pizza boxes on the kitchen table and was doling out paper plates and napkins by the time her husband and sister-in-law entered. J.C. chattered away, helping his aunt, tickling the baby's chin, giving his mother a hug in passing.

It was a pleasant family scene, and yet Jenny found she wasn't in the mood for it. She had too much to think about to truly relax and enjoy herself. Every time she looked at J.C. she felt a pang of worry, although she tried to hide it.

They ate, they talked about all the mundane family matters of interest and import only to those they loved. J.C. ate three big slices of cheese pizza, then asked to be excused so he could build a "bug house" for the collection he'd caught at the baby-sitter's. When he'd gone, Jenny sighed and leaned back in her chair. She hadn't even realized how tense she'd been, watching her son...Cole Stadler's son.

Lark offered the baby another chunk of pizza crust to chew on. "So," she said as if she'd been waiting for her chance, "did you have a nice lunch?"

Jenny wanted to groan but didn't. "It was all right," she said noncommittally.

"Faith told me that was your new boss."

Jenny devoutly wished her co-worker had minded her own business. "That's right."

"What's his name?" Jared asked, leaning an elbow on the table.

"Cole Stadler." Jenny thanked her lucky stars that she'd never told him her son's real middle name or the jig would be up. "Apparently his father owns a chain of historic hotels throughout this country and Europe."

Jared frowned. "He took you to lunch? Don't tell me he's already trying to hit on you."

"No, of course not." The conversation was making Jenny more and more uncomfortable. "He's...interested in local history, that's all. In fact, just before quitting time he was asking me all kinds of questions about our local ghosts."

"He's really great-looking," Lark said suddenly. "Smooth—"

Jared grimaced. "Like the guys you knew back in Florida? Com'on, Lark, Jenny's not interested in some smooth operator from back east."

"How do you know what your sister is interested in? You'd find something wrong with Prince Charming!"

They both looked at Jenny, waiting for her to jump into the fray. Instead, she said helplessly, "He's not from back east. He's from California."

Lark burst out laughing but Jared looked thoughtful.

"If he gives you any trouble, you let me know," he said. "I mean it."

"I know you do, and I appreciate it. But there won't be any trouble." Please, Jenny added a prayer, don't let there be any trouble! "Uh...Jared, I was wondering...."

"Yes?"

"If your invitation still stands for J.C. to spend some time with you and Lark at the ranch—"

"Oh, Jenny, that would be wonderful!" Lark leaned forward enthusiastically. "We'd love to have him with us, for just as long as you'll let him come. Jared's bought a pony—did he tell you?"

Jenny smiled. "No, but I'm not surprised." Jared had to be the best brother around, with but one little flaw: he tended to take over everyone he loved, including his sister and nephew.

"Anytime you say," Jared agreed. "How about now? We could just load him up in the car and—"

"No, no." Jenny held up her hands to slow everything down. Maybe it wouldn't be necessary at all. If Cole kept their relationship strictly business, then perhaps he'd *never* find out about the boy. "I haven't figured out the timing yet," she admitted. "As soon as I do, I'll give you a call."

They accepted that, and the conversation turned to other matters: the calf crop at Wolf Ranch, maintenance work at Wolf Cabin, which was even higher up into the mountains, the deterioration of wooden play equipment Jared had installed for J.C. a couple of years ago. Jenny tried to concentrate on what was being said but found it practically impossible.

Cole Stadler was on her mind and she simply couldn't dislodge him. For the first time she could remember, she found herself wishing Jared and Lark would cut short their visit.

At last they stood up to go. Lark gave Jenny a final hug. "Are you sure everything's all right, honey?"

"Fine. Just fine."

Lark didn't look convinced. "If you say so, but you've seemed a little...distracted this evening. We didn't keep you from something, did we? I keep telling Jared we should call before we just drop in—"

"No, of course not! You're always welcome."

And they were...but a little less tonight than usual.

When they'd gone, Jenny straightened the kitchen before calling J.C. in from the yard where he'd built his "bug house" out of a glass jar with nail holes poked in the lid. His toys were strewn from one end of the house to the other, and in keeping with family rules, it was his job to pick them up and put them away.

This he did with much dawdling and many complaints, ending with, "Who picked up all the toys before you got me, Mom?"

Jenny hauled him into her arms for a big hug while making the expected answer. "Before I got you, I didn't *have* any toys!" They laughed together and she felt emotional tears leap to her eyes. J.C. was the most precious thing in her life and, in fact, she loved him more than life itself. She'd do anything to protect him: anything!

Swallowing hard, she held him away from her. "Com'on, buster, let's get you a bath and then I'll read to you, okay?"

"I'm not dirty," he protested, looking down at a grubby T-shirt and shorts covered with dust and dirt. He made a few inconsequential swipes with his hands, then followed happily when she went to run his bath.

She thought she'd never get him to bed, but finally he was tucked in securely with repeated warnings that tomorrow Mama absolutely *had* to get to work on time.

"I promise, Mama," he said, looking at her with earnest golden eyes that nearly broke her heart.

She smoothed the damp hair back from his brow. "I was talking to Uncle Jared and Aunt Lark and they were wondering if you'd like to come spend a few days with them at the ranch this summer."

His eyelids drifted down, silky lashes touching his cheeks. "And baby Gray, too?"

"Baby Gray, too."

"But you'd be lonesome without me." He said it with perfect confidence that it was true.

"Of course, but part of learning to be a big kid is being separated from your mother...a little bit." She gave him a fierce hug.

"You're squashing me, Mama!"

"Sorry." She released him, smoothed the sheet around his shoulders and stood up. "We'll think about it, okay?"

"Okay." It came out on a sleepy yawn.

She slipped into the hall, closing his door quietly behind her. It would be good for him to spend time with his aunt and uncle, but she dreaded the thought of coming home to an empty house. That five-year-old boy filled her life with love and meaning. She would always be grateful to Cole for that if nothing—

A brisk knock on the front door halted her in midstep. Frowning, she turned to answer the summons. It was after nine o'clock, so who could be calling—

She swung open the door and looked straight into the golden eyes of Cole Stadler.

"What are you doing here?"

"Not simply passing by, you can bet on that."

He stalked inside, turning in the middle of the room to face her. He wore faded denims and a soft knit shirt, with white leather sneakers on his feet. In fact, he looked very much like the man she'd met and fallen in love with on the cruise ship.

"How did you find me?"

"It wasn't hard."

"Then *why* did you find me?"

"I had to."

"You *didn't*." She shook her head wearily. "Wasn't it hard enough all day long at the hotel? You can't just barge into my home and start tormenting me—"

"Tormenting you? I don't think so."

Before she could respond, he took the four long strides separating them and reached out to grasp her by the waist. He held her there before him, his hands like iron. She stared into his face, all rational thought blasted aside. Even when he pulled her flat against him she couldn't move a muscle in resistance.

A humorless smile touched his well-shaped mouth. "Who's tormenting whom?" he asked, and kissed her.

At the first touch of his mouth on hers, Jenny felt as if she'd been yanked through a time warp. Nothing had changed, not a single thing. His kiss still awakened in her feelings she'd never thought to confront again. His body was as lean and hard as she remembered, and her own felt completely incapable of resisting the languorous spread of heat to every extremity.

He cupped her face with both hands and angled her face just the way he wanted, the way that matched his so perfectly. Lost in a glow of sensuality, Jenny touched his waist with her hands, lightly...experimentally, as if to find out whether that, too, was the same.

And then she wrapped her arms around him and hung on, for where he was taking her she'd never gone without him for her guide. It was like the first time he had ever kissed her, in that it was such a stunning shock to her entire system. But unlike that first time more than five years ago, she knew now where this kind of surrender could lead.

Still, she didn't have it in her to resist when he drew her to the sofa and down into its depths, without ever taking his mouth from hers.

Lost in his kiss, she couldn't find a shred of resistance. With his hands roving over her, his mouth trailing kisses down her throat, she felt as if he'd stripped her of her will in a few short seconds.

He shifted over her and she moved to accommodate him. He let out a short exclamation of surprise and she felt him flinch, then saw him reach into the crease between the couch cushions to pull out—

One of J.C.'s books! Jenny lunged for it but Cole held it beyond her reach. She saw the frown creasing his forehead while he turned the oversize storybook over to look at its cover.

And then he flung it across the room. His slashing glance chilled her to her very toes.

"So you have a child," he said in a deadly tone. "Does that also mean you have a husband? Is he back there—" he jerked his head toward the hallway "—sleeping while you entertain—"

With a cry of outrage, she bucked beneath him, managing to slip from the couch before he could catch his balance. Trembling, on the verge of total collapse, she hugged her arms around her torso and tried to calm herself. When she thought she could do so without shrieking, she spoke.

"No husband."

He slid around to sit on the couch, smoothing back his dark hair with both hands. "Oh, really."

The tone was insulting to say the least, but Jenny was too terrified to challenge him on it. J.C. slept just a few feet away. Under no circumstances could she allow Cole to discover that he had a son.

His face seemed carved of granite. "Boy or girl?"

"That's really none of your business."

"Most people don't take offense at such a simple and obvious question." He cocked his head and looked at her without warmth. "What are you hiding, Geneva? Is there more than one?"

Terrified by his probing expression, Jenny cast about for some way to throw him off the track. Without conscious decision, she settled on the obvious. "Why are you giving me the third degree, Cole? You're the one who's married."

She watched the color drain from his face. He stood up, his movements jerky where before they'd been graceful and easy. She straightened her shoulders, refusing to flinch before the dark fury of his gaze. "How many children do *you* have?" she challenged him.

For a moment, he simply stared at her. Then he said, "None...now."

And without another word, he brushed past her and out of her little house.

For a long time, Jenny stood there trembling. Her mouth felt bruised from his kisses and her body tingled with the memory of his touch, imprinted years ago and brought back now with a vengeance.

Something had just happened here that she didn't understand. Whatever it was, she dared not take a chance on letting Cole see J.C. and perhaps guessing the truth.

What would Cole's reaction be? Denial? Anger? Disappointment?

Possessiveness?

J.C. stumbled into the kitchen the next morning, rubbing his eyes with one fist. "See, Mama?" he mumbled. "I told you I'd hurry."

Jenny gave him a hug. "You're my best boy, J.C. I really appreciate it—but our plans have changed a little."

"Yeah?" He almost knocked over his chair, getting his drowsy self seated. He scooted his bowl of cereal closer, then picked up his spoon.

Jenny poured the milk. "I've decided that you deserve a special treat so I'm taking you to Aunt Lark's and Uncle Jared's today for a little vacation fun. How does that sound to you?"

J.C. blinked owlishly. "I thought—"

"I know, sweetheart, but I've got to grow up someday, don't I? I know I'm going to miss you something awful, but I'll come see you on my days off. It'll help, knowing you're having a wonderful time—and you will, wait and see if you don't."

"Oh, sure." J.C. shoveled a spoonful of multicolored cereal nuggets into his mouth. "I'm not worried about *that*. I'm worried about you."

He sounded so grown-up when he said it, like the man of the house. Jenny blinked furiously to keep tears at bay.

She was doing this for him, because she loved him. They'd never been separated overnight before but she'd just have to be brave. His clothes were packed, she'd already called in sick at the Miner's Repose, and she'd spoken to Lark, who'd been surprised but pleased.

Jenny couldn't falter now, with so much at stake.

CHAPTER FOUR

CRIPPLE Creek lay in the rosy glow of dusk by the time Jenny drove back down the mountain that evening. With J.C. happily ensconced with his aunt and uncle, she felt an enormous sense of relief. He was safe, at least for the time being. She'd use this reprieve to try to figure out what she should do next.

Much depended upon Cole. Surely he wouldn't remain in Colorado indefinitely. As the son and heir of the hotel chain's founder, there must be far more important things for him to do than guide the fortunes of one small insignificant cog in an international chain. He'd do whatever he'd come to do—probably just make sure the Miner's Repose got off to a good start and perhaps approve a few of the improvement projects Mr. Grover had planned but been unable to finance. Then Cole would move on to bigger and better things.

And if she kept her wits about her, he would move on without being any the wiser about the existence of Jared Cole Wolf.

Jenny parked the little car in front of her house and hurried across the yard toward the porch, already cast into shadow by the lowering sun. She still had a lot to do to prepare for work tomorrow, since she'd been gone since early morning. She thought she had a clean blouse but she'd have to iron it and—

Just as her foot touched the bottom step, a deep voice emerged from the shadows.

"Strike two."

She flinched. Only a lucky grab for the stair railing saved her from falling. "Who—?"

Cole Stadler stepped forward. He wore running costume: shorts, T-shirt, leather sneakers reminiscent of his workout garb on board the *Inamorata II*. Jenny's breath caught in her chest and she stared up at him helplessly.

"Strike two," he repeated. "You don't look sick to me, Jenny Wolf. In fact, you look—" his gaze flicked over her, from head to foot "—pretty damned good."

This was one eventuality for which she was totally unprepared and she found herself stammering. "W-what are you doing here? You scared me to death, Cole. You have n-no right to make yourself at home on my front porch when—"

"Where have you been all day, Jenny?"

"None of your business!" Stalking past him, she tried to fit her key into the lock with hands that trembled violently.

He reached past her and took the key, his fingers brushing hers and sending little sparks of awareness careening along to her nerve endings. She gave in without a struggle, standing helplessly by while he opened her door with a flourish.

She walked inside with every intention of slamming the door in his face, but he was not to be denied. Easily blocking the door with a shoulder, he raised one brow.

"Temper, temper," he said mildly. "Little Jenny's been a bad girl—twice in two days. At this rate, you'll be on the unemployment line before we even have a chance to get... reacquainted."

She didn't like the way he said that word: *reacquainted*. She had a very strong suspicion he meant something else entirely. She turned away from him, trying desperately to come up with some plausible lie.

"I'm waiting," he reminded her.

His hands settled on her shoulders and she stiffened. Every time he touched her, she felt herself weaken even more. "I had... a personal errand to take care of," she said at last.

"A personal errand. One that took all day?"

"Yes!" She dipped her shoulders and stepped away from him, turning to forestall any further intimacy. "I'm sorry, Cole. But I'm scarcely ever ill so I thought that just this once, it wouldn't hurt if I fudged a little bit."

He cocked his head, his tawny gaze steady. "Couldn't you have tried the truth?"

"Look who's talking!"

It was the wrong thing to say; she saw his eyes turn dark and turbulent.

"What's that supposed to mean?" he demanded.

"Let it go." She turned away; a mistake, for he stopped her by catching her shoulders again. "Don't, Cole. You can't keep grabbing me every time you feel like it."

"Why not? I like touching you... and you like being touched. I want to know what you meant by that crack."

"The obvious. I wasn't the one who concealed an engagement." She lifted her chin. "And I wasn't the one who married someone else before my Caribbean tan faded."

"No," he agreed softly, "you were the one who forgot how to use a telephone."

"I explained—"

"And I don't believe you."

"Then *ask your wife.*"

He recoiled as if she'd struck him. "I can't," he said with icy calm. "She's dead."

"Oh, no—" Jenny lifted her hands instinctively, wanting to offer comfort. He looked so suddenly haggard that she supposed he hadn't been able to get over his loss. The knot in her stomach tightened even more. What they'd shared on the ship must have been a cheap diversion, since this man was obviously grieving the loss of a deeper love. "I'm so sorry," she managed to add.

"You know," he said slowly, "I believe you are."

"Is that why you came to Cripple Creek?"

"You mean, because she died and I'm trying to forget?" He frowned. "I never thought of it that way, but you could be right. She died a couple of years ago, actually. Until then, I was one of those people with a blueprint for my life. After the fire—well, everything seemed to go to pieces."

She'd never seen him look so vulnerable. Her heart went out to him in his pain, and she found herself wondering if perhaps she might hold the key to easing the grief so obvious in his face. Would the knowledge that he had a son lighten his load or make it heavier? Maybe she was wrong to keep his son's existence from him—

"My son died with his mother."

All Jenny's sympathy turned to horror. Before she could fully digest this bit of information, he went on in a tone so harsh that it sent little wavelets of apprehension skittering up her spine.

"Lynette and I had worked very hard to make our marriage...viable. But I loved that boy without reservation. If I am ever fortunate enough to have another, I swear to God I'll protect him from anything and everything—with my *life*, if need be."

The way he said it left no room for doubt, and Jenny saw the handwriting on the wall. If he learned about J.C., he would assert a father's rights—maybe even try to take the boy from her. It was a risk she could never run, not even to ease Cole's suffering.

"I'm sorry," she said helplessly, knowing mere words were inadequate. "I can't imagine how horrible it would be to lose a child."

Cole sucked in a deep breath. "But you have a child. At least tell me if you have a boy or a girl."

She licked her lips. "What difference does it make?"

"None, to me. I'd think it would make a difference to you."

She gave him a small, grudging smile. "I don't want you mixed up in my personal business, Cole. You're my boss, period."

"I'm your boss but you've never been successful in putting periods to our relationship—and in all honesty, neither have I. Quit being coy—boy or girl?"

Was that suspicion on his face? "A boy," she admitted with reluctance.

"How old is he?"

She'd wondered what she'd say if he ever had occasion to ask that question. She swallowed hard. "He's...three. Three-and-a-half, actually." *Liar*.

"I'd like to meet him someday." He glanced around. "Where've you got him stashed?"

That was exactly what she'd done; stashed him where he'd be safe. "He's visiting his aunt and uncle," she said tersely.

"What's his name?"

She turned abruptly away. "Why are you giving me the third degree?"

"All I asked was his name. What's so terrible about that?"

What, indeed. "Jared C-Charles," she said through numb lips, "but we call him J.C."

"I see."

The sadness in his tone tore at her heart. What had his son's name been? But she wouldn't ask. It obviously hurt him to talk about it. For that matter, it hurt her, too. She steeled herself to face him with head held high.

"I really do apologize for missing work today. I *am* a good employee. I promise I won't do it again."

"All right." His tone and expression revealed neither approval nor disapproval.

"Now I think you'd better go."

She expected an argument but didn't get one. He simply nodded and said, "You're right." But he didn't move.

"Now," she urged, glancing pointedly at the door. "And in the future, Cole...I hope you don't think you can just drop by anytime you feel like it."

"Why not? It's hardly as if we're strangers."

"But it's also not as if we're—we're *friends*. I have a life—"

"With a man in it?" His amber eyes narrowed to dangerous slits. "Somehow I never considered that possibility."

"What do you think I've been doing for the last five or six years, pining away for you?" She had, but she'd die before admitting it.

"Obviously not, since you have a child. By the way, you didn't tell me who Jared's father is."

"That's none of your business. I'm shocked you'd ask."

"Whoever he is, you must have loved him."

"I must have." She felt hot color flood her cheeks.

"Do you still?"

Jenny wanted to groan in frustration. He had no right to ask that question. "I'm not going to talk to you about this," she declared. "Our relationship has to be strictly business."

"Why?"

"B-because—" *Because you think I betrayed you; because if I let you get close to me again, you'll find out about J.C. and that would open an entire Pandora's box of problems.*

He cupped her quivering chin with one hand and stared down at her with a faint grin curving his sensuous mouth. "Because you missed me and you still want me, just as I missed and still want you. And I'm going to have you again, Jenny Wolf or Geneva Lupo or whatever you're calling yourself this week. And I'm not going to wait forever to do it, either."

He brought his mouth crashing down on hers in a quick, hard kiss that spread liquid fire through her veins. Just as quickly, he released her and was gone, leaving her standing there alone in the middle of her living room wrestling with the sure and certain knowledge that she was in a *lot* of trouble.

It took Cole three days—just three days!—to win over the entire staff of the Miner's Repose Hotel. Jenny saw it happen and *still* couldn't believe how he turned on the charm.

He treated everyone with unfailing courtesy and respect, but Mr. Grover had done that, too. What really turned the tide in Cole's favor was a staff meeting at which he announced his plans for the old hotel.

Even Jenny was impressed. Everything Mr. Grover had planned and dreamed of but been unable to finance, Cole and World Heritage Hotels would achieve.

"And that includes renovations to the bridal suite, where I understand the resident ghosts hang out." Cole grinned at the assembled employees. "I'm hoping all the workmen won't discourage them, since they add a certain charm to the old place. That'll be the final phase of our plans, however. In the meantime I'll continue to live there while I look for something more permanent."

His secretary looked dubious. "When's all this supposed to start, Mr. Stadler?"

"Interior and exterior construction will begin in October, when the tourist season starts winding down. Everything will be done in strict accordance to standards of historical preservation."

A brief but enthusiastic smattering of applause greeted this pronouncement.

Cole nodded. "And starting immediately, I'm doubling your clothing allowance and picking up the tab for costume maintenance. Before I'm finished, the Miner's Repose is going to be the most desirable place to work in Cripple Creek—and the most desirable place to stay. We'll be refurbishing all the rooms and redecorating to stress the historical aspects. With that in mind—"

His smiling gaze sought and found Jenny, who resisted an urge to sink down into her seat.

"Miss Wolf, will you remain after this meeting is concluded? Since you seem to be the resident expert on all things historical, I'd like to bring you in on my plans and get your input."

Everybody was looking at her. She sighed. "I have duty at the registration desk, Mr. Stadler. Perhaps another time—"

She was painfully aware of the gasp of disbelief her words elicited.

"Perhaps *now*." His suddenly hard glance bored into her. "I'm sure my secretary can find someone to handle your chores, since I deem your participation in the preservation of hotel history to be a top priority."

Nona nodded with enthusiasm. "Absolutely. Don't you worry about a thing, Mr. Stadler. I'll see that everything is covered."

"Excellent. Now if there are no further questions, this meeting is adjourned."

The meeting room emptied out around Jenny, who remained seated while trying to ignore curious glances cast in her direction. When they were alone, Cole walked to the end of the row where she sat and put one hand on the back of a chair.

"You got a problem with my plans?" he asked innocently.

"That depends on which plans you're talking about," she retorted.

He grinned. "First things first. I'm talking about the hotel, of course."

"About that," she said, "I'm thrilled."

"You're thrilled about all my plans," he said bluntly. "Don't deny it, Jenny."

She lifted her chin. "I won't dignify that with an answer."

"Because one isn't necessary." He gestured with the curling fingers of one hand. "Come along."

Instant alarm flashed through her. "Come along where?"

"To my suite for lunch. We may as well be comfortable while we talk."

"In your suite? I don't think so!"

"Don't be ridiculous. You want to see what the bridal suite looks like, don't you?"

"Well . . . I *am* curious. But—"

"No buts. You'll be perfectly safe—check that. You'll be as safe as you want to be." He held out his hand.

She started to take it, then pulled back her own hand. Touching him was dangerous under any circumstances and she'd avoid it if she could. But she couldn't very well avoid lunch and conversation about her almost-favorite subject, the Miner's Repose Hotel.

Jenny had been inside the bridal suite at the Miner's Repose only once, and that had been shortly after she went to work at the hotel. She'd had to plead with Mr. Grover to let her in, for the place was in such bad shape that he'd been concerned about injuries and lawsuits.

Now she found it vastly improved, if still Spartan in its decor. She, and everyone else who worked here, had known some limited amount of renovation was under way, but they hadn't realized it was aimed at turning the suite into a livable environment for the new owner.

The suite, as she remembered, consisted of a sitting room, a bedroom and private bath—quite a luxury, for few rooms in the Miner's Repose could boast such a twentieth-century amenity. The Oriental carpet, original to the hotel, had been cleaned. When she saw its jewel-like tones, she knelt to stroke her hand across the surface flattened by wear.

"This is lovely," she said, looking up at Cole. "I'm so glad it could be salvaged."

He nodded, his expression thoughtful. "Lovely things should always be salvaged, if there's any way at all it can be done."

Jenny gave him an uncertain smile before rising to look around with keen interest. A round table draped in lacy layers of snowy white stood near a bow window, rays of sunshine slanting across its surface. Two place settings of sparkling crystal and china were already in place, as was a cut-glass bud vase holding a graceful apricot-colored rose.

There was nothing else in the room, except for a small horsehair-covered settee and a chair with cracked leather upholstery, set near a marble fireplace.

He waited until her glance skittered past the door leading to the bedroom before asking, "Would you care to see the rest of it?"

She caught her breath but tried to respond as casually as he. "Of course . . . but not just now. We have work to do, after all. Another time."

He nodded, one corner of his well-shaped mouth tilting up. "Whatever you say. Another time. You can count on it."

A light rapping on the door behind them announced the arrival of their lunch. One of the waiters from the restaurant wheeled in his cart with a flourish.

"I think you'll find everything to your satisfaction," he told Cole. He deposited a silver wine

bucket on a stand, which he moved to an incon-
spicuous spot near one chair. "Only the finest
and freshest, as you requested, sir."

"I'm sure it will do," Cole agreed, sounding
almost bored. After the waiter had withdrawn,
Cole pulled out a chair and nodded at Jenny.
"May I?"

Feeling helpless, she allowed him to seat her,
then watched him take his own place and drop a
snowy linen napkin into his lap. "Wine?" He
lifted the bottle from the bucket.

She shook her head resolutely. "I never have
wine with lunch. It makes me sleepy."

He poured wine into two glasses and placed
one before her. "If you get sleepy this afternoon,
I give you permission to come up here and take
a nap." He lifted his fragile crystal glass.
"Cheers."

Still she hesitated. "Really, there are very few
wines I like."

"And this is one of them—chardonnay. Did
you think I'd forgotten?"

She was beginning to suspect he might remember everything as clearly as she did. In that
case— "Cheers." Touching her glass lightly to
his, she drank.

He seemed satisfied. "I took the liberty of or-
dering for us both," he said, although that was
obvious. "I hope you enjoy your salad."

It was one of the most beautiful salads she'd
ever seen, certainly far superior to the bag of raw
veggies she kept in the hotel refrigerator for quick
lunches. Displayed in an elegant crystal bowl, this
salad boasted a variety of greens topped with tiny

asparagus spears—again, her favorite—plus strips of roasted chicken accompanied by toasty golden-brown breadsticks.

Her first bite was not a disappointment. "It tastes as good as it looks," she admitted. "But you really didn't need to go to all this bother."

"You're worth a certain amount of bother." He spoke as casually as if he, too, were commenting on the food. "Dessert will also be special."

Her antenna went up. If he thought *she* was going to be dessert— "Yes?"

His smile radiated innocence. "Strawberries. Fresh, sweet strawberries."

She closed her eyes, remembering another time they'd shared strawberries...and wine...and apricot-colored roses. "So tell me what you have in mind for this history preservation project," she choked. "After all, you invited me here for a r-reason."

"Oh, yes," he agreed softly. "I certainly did...."

Jenny found lunch an absolutely excruciating affair. The food was delicious and her companion didn't say a single word which she could take amiss, yet she found it impossible to concentrate on the conversation. He somehow managed to turn the simple act of eating into a sensual display that had her constantly licking her lips and catching her breath, especially at the sight of a ripe, juicy strawberry disappearing into an equally sweet mouth.

Only the barest outline of his proposal sunk in: that he hoped to use photographs and antiques and brass information plates engraved in turn-of-the-century style to entice guests to enter into the spirit of those times.

"Of course, we can also use multimedia if we decide it's appropriate," he said, leaning back in his chair. "But I'm not too sure about that aspect. Would it be better to stick to the technology of the period? Or should we pull out all the stops and use everything civilization has come up with since?" He cocked his head quizzically. "What do you think, Jenny?"

His question flustered her, since she'd been concentrating on *him*, not what he was saying. "W-why, I don't know."

"Does that mean you have to think about it?"

She leapt at the out he'd conveniently provided. "Exactly." She dropped her napkin on the table and stood up. "It's been a lovely lunch, really it has, but now I've got to get back to work."

He stood, too. "Not so fast. You haven't seen the rest of the suite."

She edged toward the door. "Some other time, all right?"

"Not all right. Now."

That was his "boss" voice, and it caused her to hesitate.

His tone gentled. "You look so at home here, Jenny. You seem completely comfortable in period costume." He touched her elbow lightly, but with purpose.

"I love wearing these clothes." She smoothed her dark skirt and took a breath so deep that the lacy ruffles across her breast rose trembling. "All except the shoes." She poked a pointed kidskin-covered toe from beneath her hem.

He looked startled. "I should have remembered your penchant for going barefoot. You can take your shoes off when you're with me. Sit down and I'll help you."

"Oh, good heavens, no!" She backed away from him, appalled at the hot rise of color she felt in her cheeks.

He followed slowly but with determination. "In fact, when you're with me...you can take off anything you like."

She bumped into the door and reached around to scrabble for the knob with one hand. "There's not a single thing I want to take off, down to and including my shoes. I told you, this is a business relationship."

"In your dreams."

His face swooped down on hers, blotting out the room and the place and even the century. Pressed between the closed door and his iron-hard chest, Jenny had nowhere to run...and when his lips touched hers, she knew she didn't want to run at all. He tasted of strawberries and chardonnay, of memories and regrets. She found herself clinging to him, her arms around his neck and her eyes tightly closed.

He trailed kisses across her cheek to her ear. "Now might be a perfect time to show you the other room," he murmured, his warm breath stirring the tendrils of dark hair escaping from the bun atop her head.

"The—?" Her eyes blinked open just as understanding sank in. "You rat!" She gave him a shove.

He allowed her to push him away, and he was smiling. "Well?" he challenged, a devilish glint in his golden eyes. "You might as well, Jenny Wolf. Why delay the inevitable...unless you think anticipation will make your eventual surrender even sweeter." He touched her shoulder possessively. "Come into the other room with me, Jenny, my sweet."

"Not now and not ever! I told you, we're not going to start up again."

"Yes, we are."

"How can I get this through your head?" At last she found the doorknob and her hand closed over it. "I'm not going to tumble into your bed at the drop of a hat."

"You did once."

"I was young and foolish then!"

He arched one brow. "How young?"

She'd gone to great lengths to mislead him about that. Perhaps this was time for the truth. She lifted her chin and stared into his eyes. "I was twenty."

That rocked him, but then she saw another thought forming in his mind. "Twenty...and a virgin. Damn it, you *were* a virgin! You denied it and I let you, because I didn't want it to be true, but—"

She yanked open the door. "That's over and done with. Forget it, Cole. It wasn't important then and it's not important now."

"Oh, no?"

His voice pursued her to the stairway.

"That's what you think, Geneva Lupo!"

CHAPTER FIVE

"Jenny, dear, Mr. Stadler would like to see you in his office right away."

Balancing the telephone handset on one shoulder, Jenny groaned and closed the registration book with a snap that nearly knocked it off the counter. "Not again!" she begged. Cole summoned her to his office a half dozen times a day, and had ever since he'd taken over almost two weeks ago. Everyone who worked at the Miner's Repose had noticed and was talking about it; worse, he didn't seem to mind the gossip in the slightest.

Nona's warm chuckle came across the wire. "Must be something good! You haven't been late since that first day he arrived."

That was true, but probably only because J.C. was still visiting his aunt and uncle. Jenny sighed. "All right, Nona. Tell him I'll be right there." Hanging up, she glanced at Faith, her co-worker. "I'm sorry, but the boss wants to see me."

Faith grinned. "Don't pretend that's a hardship. I should be so lucky, Jenny Wolf."

Jenny didn't consider it lucky. Cole was driving her crazy, and she knew it was deliberate. He looked at her as if she were an ice cream cone on a hot summer day, and he never missed an opportunity to touch her—accidentally, of course. He tried to entice her to lunch, to dinner, to tour

77

his suite, but she knew what he was really after... her body.

Well, he wasn't going to get it! He was a constant threat to her self-control but an even more dangerous threat to her dearest love: her son. He hadn't believed her explanation of her failure to contact him after the cruise, and as a result he obviously didn't trust her. If he ever realized that she'd kept from him one of the most important pieces of information a man could ever receive, he'd despise her.

And then he'd take her child from her, just as surely as she lived and breathed. Squaring her shoulders, she knocked on his door with firm strokes, then waited for his invitation to "Come in."

His smile was dazzling. "I made some notes about our historical preservation plans and I thought perhaps we could discuss them tonight over dinner."

"I'm sorry," she said, her face stiff, "but I have other plans."

His golden eyes narrowed. "Change them."

"I can't."

"Can't or won't?"

"It amounts to the same thing, doesn't it?"

"Well, hell." Turning, he tossed several folders onto his desk, then slanted a dark glance in her direction. "I'd be careful if I were you. I tend to surliness when I get too frustrated."

"I refuse to accept any responsibility whatsoever for your level of frustration." Jenny drew in a deep breath and lifted her chin. "If that's all—"

"No, Geneva, it's not all." He advanced and she retreated, step for step. "You're making this unnecessarily difficult, you know. There's no reason we can't pick up where we left off."

No reason that he knew of. "We can't go back, Cole."

"Sure we can."

She reached the wall and had nowhere else to retreat. Reaching out, he stroked her set jaw with his hand. She arched her neck and turned her head away, a traitorous part of her wanting to purr with satisfaction as his fingers slid up behind her sensitive ear.

Leaning forward, he pressed his lips to the throbbing pulse in her forehead. "You want me, Jenny. Why are you fighting it?"

"I want you...to leave me alone!" Bracing her hands on his muscular biceps, she pushed him away. She was breathing hard and she felt tendrils of hair against her cheeks, tendrils he'd dislodged. "Don't do this to me, Cole! We can never regain what we lost. Times change, people change—"

"But some things remain the same." He didn't try to touch her but he didn't have to; his steady, burning gaze kept her anchored before him. "What we feel for each other...physically, at least, hasn't changed at all. If anything, it's grown stronger."

She groaned. "Nooo—"

"Yes, Jenny. We're older and, we can only hope, wiser. This time we'll both go in with our eyes wide open. There won't be the usual strings attached—strings about love and commitment and happily-ever-after. That's the part of our relationship that failed, not the act of love itself.''

Jenny pressed back against the wall, exquisitely aware of the rush of blood through her veins. Somehow this man made her feel more intensely alive than she had ever imagined she could be. But even without J.C. to consider, she knew she couldn't possibly fall into line with his plans for their future.

He'd broken her heart once and she wasn't going to let him do it again. With a conscious act of will, she straightened. ''There are always strings attached, whether we plan it that way or not. I'm not interested in a cheap affair with—''

''Cheap?'' He looked astounded, his brows arching in his lean face. ''No affair with me could ever be classified as *cheap*. You should remember that from our last love affair.''

It hurt her terribly to hear him call it that. ''First *and* last,'' she forced herself to say. ''Find someone else to—to bedevil! There are plenty of candidates for the position. Just *leave me alone*.''

He let her walk out of his office and close the door, but even with a solid wall between them he didn't let her stop thinking about him...and thinking about him...and thinking about him.

The telephone on Jenny's bedside table rang and she lunged for it with a mother's first thought: something's wrong with my child! But the voice that answered her anxious ''Hello?'' was rich and deep and sexy.

''Hello, Geneva. Did I wake you?''

Instead of calming down, her heart raced even faster. "N-no, I was reading." She glanced at her alarm clock and saw that it was nearly eleven o'clock. "Is something wrong?"

"Yes, and you know what it is."

Alone in her own bedroom, she felt heat in her cheeks...in the pit of her belly. "Is this about to deteriorate into an obscene phone call? Because if it is—"

"Hold it!" His laughter, warm and dark and sweet as hot fudge, made her shiver. "Actually, there's another reason for this call. I'm going to Denver tomorrow and I thought you might like to come along."

"No way!" She sat up in bed, shoving a pillow between her back and the headboard.

"Even if we do a few of the historical sites while we're there? I thought we might check out LoDo—"

Lower Downtown, she translated, where old businesses and warehouses had been refurbished into some of the toniest and most desirable addresses in Denver.

"—and the Molly Brown house, a few of the other attractions."

"It's tempting," she lied, "but I've already—"

"Been there, done that, huh. I guess the company wouldn't make it worth repeating yourself."

"It's the company I'm trying to avoid," she said tartly. "Really, Cole—"

"Are you in bed?"

"W-why—" She glanced down at her faded cotton T-shirt, frowning. "Yes, but I don't see what that—"

"Grow up, Jenny!" Again that high-calorie laughter. "I guess I'll just have to do Denver all alone. Sleep tight, sweetheart—and dream of me."

The click of his hang-up jarred her from her lethargy. Just hearing his voice seemed to turn her blood to molasses, moving heavy and sweet through her veins.

Damn him! He was playing a game but she couldn't afford that. If he kept this up he was going to get far more than he bargained for.

Laying her book aside, Jenny squeezed her eyes closed. It was time to face facts, and the most important fact was, Cole Stadler was still in her blood. If she didn't get away from him, she was going to end up back in his bed.

She couldn't let that happen and there was only one way she could see to avoid it. She had to leave.

She must take J.C. away, far away, where Cole Stadler would never find them. She'd have to go without giving notice, just disappear. She'd have to start a new life for herself and her son.

Lying there in the dark, she reviewed her resources even though she knew what she'd find. She didn't have nearly enough money to pull this off. If she sold the ring she now knew to be a diamond—

No! The ring was for J.C. She wasn't ready to sell it, not yet, so she'd have to go to her brother for help. She'd have to find a way to approach him, though.

If Jared found out about Cole's relationship to J.C., it would be almost as bad as Cole himself finding out. Jared was so fiercely protective that there was no telling what he might do—up to and including a showdown with the man he'd naturally assume had seduced and abandoned his baby sister.

It took Jenny a long time to fall asleep that night but by the time she had, she'd decided what she must do. Day after tomorrow—Friday—she'd call Jared and set her plan into motion.

When Cole wasn't in his office before Jenny arrived for work, she deduced with a sigh of relief that he'd gone on to Denver without her. His absence was like a load off her shoulders and she went through her day with a light step and an almost constant smile hovering around her lips.

She shared lunch in the employees' lounge with Nona, who commented on Jenny's cheerful mood.

The secretary smiled mischievously. "And I know why," she declared. "I hope you don't mind that all of us have noticed how interested Mr. Stadler is in you."

Jenny's heart plummeted, and a bite of good Miner's Repast bread turned to sawdust in her mouth. "Oh, no, he's not really. He's just—" *Just trying to get me into bed.*

Nona looked dubious, to say the least. "Com'on, Jenny, we've got eyes. The guy's crazy about you." She picked up her ham and cheese sandwich, then hesitated. "You never did mention how you knew him before."

"I didn't, did I?"

Nona laughed. "Okay, I can take a hint. But we're all rooting for something good to come of this. You're too sweet and pretty to spend the rest of your life alone." She dropped the last bite of sandwich back onto her napkin. "Not only that, J.C. needs a daddy. I think Mr. Stadler could be a good one, with a little encouragement."

"J.C.'s doing fine," Jenny said stiffly. "If he needs a role model, he'll never have a better one than his Uncle Jared."

"Com'on, Jen, an uncle's not the same as a daddy. Besides, Jared has his own son now. Not that he'll treat J.C. any different," Nona added quickly, "but the boy will know. He'll know, and it'll hurt."

Jenny bit her lip, seeing the potential for disaster multiplying before her eyes. Nona was right, J.C. did need a father. Since she dared not take a chance on the real thing, she owed it to her son to find a substitute. On the spot, she vowed that would be her first order of business, once they'd relocated.

As Nona chatted on enthusiastically about renovations at the hotel, Jenny became more and more miserable because she knew she wouldn't be around to see the completed project. If only someone other than Cole Stadler and his family had bought the hotel; if only someone other than Cole had been sent to spearhead the renovations; if only—

If only she didn't feel her resolve melting away every time he came close to her.

At five minutes to six, the front door of the Miner's Repose burst open and a small figure hurtled through. He paused in the middle of the lobby, looking around until he spotted Jenny. Then he threw himself forward.

"Mama, Mama, I've come to see you!" J.C.'s strong young arms closed around her.

He felt like heaven in her embrace. "Honey! This is a wonderful surprise!" Looking over his shoulder toward the door, she saw Jared and Lark enter, little Gray perched in a baby backpack high on his father's shoulders. All three were smiling.

J.C. straightened and took a step back, so he could peer into his mother's face. He wore cowboy boots and jeans with a plaid shirt and a felt cowboy hat shoved back at a cocky angle. His grin melted his mother's heart.

"Uncle Jared and Aunt Lark say we can take you to dinner, Mama. Is that okay? We had to come to town for supplies—" he glanced at his uncle, who nodded agreement "—so we thought we'd just kick up our heels a little before we head back up the mountain."

The voice was J.C.'s but the words were pure Jared. Jenny pulled the boy into her arms for another fierce hug before releasing him. Behind her smile, terror lurked. What if Cole walked in right now? How would she protect her secrets?

"Dinner's a great idea," she said quickly. "I'll grab my purse and we can go."

Lark nodded happily. "We thought we might eat right here in the Miner's Repast. Last time we were here, I had a chocolate torte for dessert that was out of this world."

"Not here," Jenny objected. "Let's go somewhere else, okay? I mean, if you don't mind." While she stumbled through her excuses, she reached behind the counter and pulled out her small purse. "Anywhere, I don't care, as long as it's not here. I spend too much time in this place."

Jared patted her shoulder. "Calm down, Jen. A simple 'I'd rather eat somewhere else' would have been sufficient."

He held the door for her and she bolted through, dragging J.C. along with her.

On the sidewalk, she felt a little safer and paused to draw a deep breath. Cole probably wouldn't be back for hours; he might even spend the night in Denver.

So why did she keep feeling he'd appear at any moment?

Together they strolled over to Bennett Avenue and up the sloping street past a solid row of gambling houses, restaurants and souvenir shops. The jingle of coins destined for slot machines drifted out onto the street, a sound so familiar that locals hardly heard it anymore. Tourists wandered around, many taking in Jenny's period garb with smiles or curious stares.

Hawkers, most also in costume, loitered in front of many of the establishments, trying to entice tourists to enter and, presumably, lose all their money. With only low-stakes gambling allowed and slot machines taking as little as a nickel, that could take a while for anyone except the most untalented—or most unlucky—of gamblers. All the hawkers nodded or spoke to Jenny, often including J.C. in their greetings.

Jared halted before a casino with an upstairs dining room known for its steaks. "This place okay?"

Lark nodded, then glanced at Jenny, who did likewise. Together they crossed the red carpet with its old-fashioned pattern and trooped up the stairs. Still nervous, Jenny kept waiting for Cole to materialize from behind a potted palm or some equally unlikely place.

But she was being paranoid, she scolded herself. Jared's and Lark's arrival was a godsend, since Jenny had to secure their support before she could put the rest of her plan into action. The sooner that was done, the better.

And then there was her joy at being reunited with her son. His hand had hardly been out of hers since they'd left the Miner's Repose. J.C. looked happy and healthy and very, very pleased to be with his mother again.

She was pleased, too.

"Anyone care for dessert?" The waitress grinned down at the remains of the feast.

In a highchair, Gray cooed and waved his spoon around in a chubby fist. He'd crumbled up enough crackers to feed an army of hungry birds, then tossed several carrot sticks and a banana after them. Gray was just reaching the stage where he insisted upon feeding himself, no matter what the consequences.

Jared was so pleased and proud of his son that he overtipped scandalously to make up for the mess. Watching father and son, Jenny sighed. She remembered when J.C. had been a baby... but he'd been a baby without the adoration of a father.

"No dessert for me," she said quickly. "I couldn't even finish my steak."

"I'll bring you a doggie bag to take it home," the waitress offered. "How about the rest'a you folks?"

Jared chose apple pie, Lark selected cheesecake, and J.C., yawning, decided on chocolate ice cream. While they waited, the boy leaned back against his corner of the booth with drooping eyelids.

Lark smiled at him fondly. "He's been working awfully hard," she confided to Jenny. "He helps with the horses, and when Jared rides out, J.C.'s right beside him."

J.C. nodded sleepily. "Uncle Jared says I've got the makin's of a real top hand. Isn't that right, Uncle Jared?"

Jared's dark face softened when he looked at his nephew. "You bet it is. Your mama can be real proud of you."

She was. While the others ate their desserts, she thought about what she wanted to say and how best to say it. She'd trust her brother with her life... but not with her secret.

J.C. finished eating first. Without urging, he slid around on the bench seat to lie down with a sigh, settling his head on his mother's lap. Absently she stroked his face, loving the smooth resilience of his little-boy cheek.

"Ahhh." Jared savored his last bite of pie and placed his fork on the table. His curious gaze locked in on his sister's face. "Is it safe to assume you're in no great hurry to leave?"

She frowned. "I—why, no, I—"

"It's obvious you have something you want to talk to us about—us, me, Lark, who? Want me to take old Gray Wolf here for a walk?"

"Or I will," Lark put in anxiously, "if this is something between brother and sister."

Jenny sighed. "You're very sweet, but actually, I want to talk to you both together." She took a deep breath. "This is completely confidential—nobody knows what I'm thinking about and I want to keep it that way."

"Now you got me curious." Jared signaled the waitress, who refilled all the coffee cups, giving Jenny time to compose herself.

When she had, she said what she had to say right out. "I want to move away from Cripple Creek and I don't have the money to do it. You've offered me financial help so many times, Jared—"

"Which you've refused, also so many times."

Jenny hung her head. "Now I'm ready to accept. I'll pay you back, I swear, but I need enough to get started somewhere else."

Lark's gaze was melting with compassion. "Where, Jenny? Where are you going?"

This was the hard part. "I...I'm not sure. Denver, Pueblo...or maybe I should try another state entirely. New Mexico's nice—"

"In other words," Jared cut in, "you're not going *to* something, you're going *away* from Cripple Creek."

"I...suppose you could say that," she admitted miserably.

"Why?"

Good old Jared never tiptoed around a question. "Lots of reasons. J.C.'s getting older, so maybe this isn't the best place for him to grow up after all, with all the gambling and so forth."

Lark frowned. "But you always said—"

"I know what I said, but now I'm saying something different. Please try to understand, Lark. It just isn't the same anymore. I think I need new challenges, new people...."

"What'a you call your new boss if he's not new people?" Jared demanded. "I noticed you didn't even mention him, or all the plans for the hotel. I thought you'd like that."

"How did you know?"

"Newspaper. Sounds like this company's got the deep pockets to pay for it, too. Not like Grover, who was all good intentions and pie in the sky."

"He did his best," Jenny protested.

Lark patted her sister-in-law's hand. "Nobody's saying he didn't, honey. But things should be even better at the Miner's Repose soon, unless..."

Jenny waited, hoping for the best. She got the worst, but it was from her brother.

"Unless the new owner's giving you a hard time," he said. "There are laws against that kind of thing, Jenny. If this guy's trying to hit on you, you don't have to quit and run.''

"That's not—'' She stopped short, then stiffened her backbone and went on. "I've got no future here. I need to make something out of myself for my son, don't you see? I need to get out, meet new men, maybe even find a father for him.'' It was true, so why did it taste like a lie? "But I can't do it alone. If you'll help me, Jared—''

He made a scornful sound. "You know I will. Tell me how much you need and I'll write the check.''

A blessed sense of relief washed over her. "I don't know yet.''

"When are you giving notice at the hotel?''

She bit her lip. "I'm not. I'm just going to go. Maybe when I take my vacation—I'll just leave a letter of resignation.''

"Damn it, Jenny!'' Baby Gray jumped in surprise and his spoon sailed out of his hand and banged against the wall. Jared handed him another without missing a syllable. "This isn't sounding right to me. I need to know—''

"I'll tell you everything you need to know, but you've got to keep quiet about my plans. I don't want *anybody* to get wind of what I'm up to.''

"I'm not sure I can go along with this. What—''

"Don't badger your sister. She has her reasons and you'll learn what they are in good—''

"Maybe I shouldn't have confided in you, Jared Wolf. I didn't ask for your advice or your blessing.''

"No, you just want my money."

"How can you say such a—"

A new voice joined the mix in a voice as silky rich as new cream, effectively cutting off Jenny's retort. "Well, well, well, what have we here?"

Jenny raised horrified eyes to meet those of Cole Stadler.

There was nothing to do but introduce him, which Jenny did with sinking heart. Jared rose and the two men stood literally toe to toe, each bearing down a tad harder on the handshake than was strictly necessary.

Which didn't surprise Jenny, since Jared was always wary where his wife or sister or anyone else he cared for was concerned. What surprised her was Lark's reaction. As sweet and trusting an individual as anyone was likely to find, she stared at Cole with the most peculiar expression on her face.

He, in turn, gave her his most charming smile. Then he glanced around, spotted an empty chair and pulled it up to the end of the booth beside the baby, where he sat without invitation. Gray promptly made a lunge for him, sticky baby fingers twisting in fine gauge knit.

Lark gasped. "Jared, don't let that baby—!"

Cole waved her off. He was smiling at Gray, and Gray smiled back, his tiny bottom tooth gleaming. "I like babies," Cole said softly. He glanced at Jenny. "I take it this one isn't yours?"

Lark laughed. "Hardly! J.C. is—"

"Much older," Jenny blurted, terrified Lark had been about to say "five years old." Jenny had told Cole her son was only ... what *had* she said? Three or four, not that it mattered. If J.C. roused and sat up where Cole could get a good look at him, her goose was cooked. Her son was big for a five-year-old and could never pass for younger.

Cole chucked Gray beneath the chin, eliciting storms of giggles. "How old's this little guy?"

"Almost ten months," the proud mother informed him. She smiled. "You're really very good with babies, Mr. Stadler."

"Call me Cole." He picked a clean spoon from the table and offered it to Gray. "I ... had a son once. I lost him when he was just a toddler."

His pain was so evident that Jenny could feel it. Lark must have, too, for she gasped and her expression turned tender.

"I'm so sorry."

"Thank you." Cole made a great pretense of looking over the edge of the table at the sleeping form curled up beside Jenny. "Is this your son, then, Jenny?"

Fighting the terror, all she could do was nod and pray that J.C. wouldn't wake up until this man had gone. "You must be in a hurry," she said quickly to Cole. "Don't let us keep you."

He frowned. "What makes you think—?"

"Didn't you just return from Denver?"

"Yes, but—"

"So you must want to get back to the hotel, find out how everything went today."

"So how *did* everything go today?"

"Uh ... fine."

"Then why," he asked, including Lark and Jared in his question, "should I rush back to find out, when you've just told me?"

"What do I know? All kinds of things might have happened and I wouldn't necessarily have a clue."

"Hey, if the place burned down, someone would have mentioned it."

Lark grinned; even Jared looked amused.

Jenny wasn't. She found herself fighting the feeling that she was loosing ground here. Worse— she felt J.C. stir on her lap, move—

She patted his back, uttering soothing little words urging him back to sleep. Helplessly she watched him yawn, stretch, sit up, rubbing his eyes.

Cole watched, too, his gaze friendly and interested. He leaned forward until his face was on a level with the boy's. "Hi," he said cheerfully. "I'm a friend of—"

The boy's eyes opened and Cole's words choked off as clear amber eyes met clear amber eyes.

CHAPTER SIX

SOMETHING hot and possessive flared in Cole's golden eyes, then was quickly shuttered. The smile he turned on Jenny was coldly mechanical. "Big boy for three," he said.

Before she could gather her wits to reply, J.C. piped up.

"I'm *almost* six," he announced. "I'm gonna be in first grade!"

"Really." Cole's expression softened when he looked at the boy. "I must have misunderstood what your mother told me. What did you say your name is?"

"I'm J.C. Who're you?"

Jenny finally recovered herself sufficiently to speak. "Watch your manners, honey. T-this is my new boss, Mr. Stadler."

"Mr. Stat—?"

"Mr. *Stadler*."

J.C. frowned. "The one who's mean to you?"

Jenny gasped. "I never said—"

Cole laughed, all his attention centered on the boy; in fact, he'd scarcely taken his gaze off J.C. since he'd awakened. "What makes you think I'm mean to your mother?"

The boy shrugged. "The first day she was late and I guess you were mean to her then. But it wasn't her fault. I couldn't find my special T-shirt." He frowned and glanced at his mother, sitting petrified beside him. "Is that why you sent me to stay with Aunt Lark and Uncle Jared, Mama, because I'm poky? If you'll let me come home again, I promise—"

"Let you!" Aghast, Jenny glanced at the aunt and uncle in question. "I thought you were having a great time at the ranch."

"I am, only..." J.C. looked sheepish. "I miss you, Mama. Can I come home now?"

Quick tears leapt to Jenny's eyes and she gave him a hug. "Of course you can." Of course; the worst had already happened and there was no longer a reason for him to stay hidden away. "Can you thank your aunt and uncle for having you visit them?"

"Yeah, thanks." He softened his perfunctory words with a big smile. "Thanks for letting me be a cowboy, Uncle Jared. Thanks for the chocolate-chip cookies, Aunt Lark."

Lark, who'd been watching with a puzzled expression, smiled at the boy. "Anytime, J.C. We love having you."

Jared frowned at his sister. "About what we were just talking about—"

"Not now," she interrupted quickly, barely stopping herself from casting a significant glance toward Cole. "There's plenty of time to discuss that. In the meantime, I think I'd better get this young man home."

"We'll bring his things the next time we're in town," Lark suggested. She still looked confused.

"That'll be fine." Jenny picked up her purse, eager to get away.

"Did you drive or walk to work this morning?" Jared asked.

That was the question she'd hoped to avoid. "I walked, but—"

"Then Lark and I will take you home."

"Then *I'll* take them home."

Everybody turned to Cole, who looked as determined as he sounded.

Jared leaned forward. "Look, Stadler, you may be Jenny's boss, but she's not at work now. I'll see her and the boy home."

Cole didn't retreat an inch. "I said, *I'll drive them home*. I've got a few things to say to your sister."

"Damn it, you can't—"

"Jared, it's all right." Jenny fought to control the panic rising into her chest.

"But you don't have to—"

"I know I don't. But now that I think of it, there are a couple of things I need to discuss with Cole—with Mr. Stadler—too. Please don't make an issue of it, all right?"

If he did, Cole looked perfectly capable of revealing a great deal more than she cared to have revealed. If she hoped to salvage anything at all from this mess, she had to keep control of the situation.

Keep control? Get control, more like it.

J.C. kept up a running commentary all the way home, encouraged by Cole's gentle urging. The boy talked about his uncle's ranch, about the horses and cattle and dogs and cats, about his little cousin, Gray, and the great cookies his Aunt Lark turned out by the dozens.

At last Cole pulled his BMW to the side of the road in front of Jenny's little house and killed the engine.

J.C. kept right on talking. "But I'm still glad to be home," he confided. "My mama needs me to take care of her, you know."

Cole glanced at Jenny, seated stiffly beside him. "I'll just bet she does," he agreed. "Doesn't your father—?"

"Got no father," J.C. put in quickly. "But I got a bicycle. You wanna see it?"

"Oh, no, J.C.!" Jenny threw open her car door. "Mr. Stadler—"

"—would love to see your bicycle, although that doesn't seem like a fair exchange for a father." Cole shot her a hostile glance.

Jenny sagged against her seat. "Don't, Cole. Don't do this. You have no right—"

"Right!" His calm facade slipped badly and the fire in his eyes made her gasp. "You dare to speak to me of *rights*?" As quickly as he'd revealed his churning emotions, he shuttered them once more. Turning to J.C. in the back seat, he grinned. "Let's go take a look at that bike, okay?"

J.C. blinked. "Okay." He cast his mother a concerned glance but when she gave him a shaky smile, he seemed ready to accept it on face value.

Cole was so tender with the boy that Jenny could barely stand to watch them together. They examined his bicycle, then J.C. pulled out his other most treasured possessions to share: the Dr. Seuss books, an array of plastic action heroes, an Indian arrowhead found on his uncle's ranch, a chunk of fool's gold from Cripple Creek.

Only he wasn't the fool, his mother was. Jenny could hardly stand to be in the same room with them, yet couldn't bear to leave them alone for a second for fear of what Cole might say.

When bedtime arrived, it was Cole who read the storybook aloud to the yawning boy. Leaning in the doorway, Jenny watched her son's father lean over and kiss the chubby cheek, then tuck the covers up around J.C.'s shoulders. Tears blurring her vision, she turned away, feeling very close to the edge of her control.

She couldn't think, couldn't plan. She'd thought Cole *knew* the moment he looked into his son's amber eyes, but perhaps that was merely her own guilty conscience at work. Maybe he *didn't* know. Maybe he'd have reacted the same to any child. Maybe she was just borrowing trouble.

She crossed the living room and stood with her forehead pressed against a cold windowpane. She could deny everything, after all. How could he prove—?

His voice, coming from behind, scourged her.

"I can almost understand how you could deprive me of my son, but how could you deprive your son of his father? I never thought you heartless, Geneva Lupo, but now I've got to wonder."

She flinched before his attack. Realizing she was in for the fight of her life, she lifted her chin and faced him. "You don't know what you're talking about, Cole. J.C. isn't—"

"Don't compound your offenses by lying to me." His amber eyes blazed in a face curiously pale beneath its even tan. "Everything fits—his age, the way he looks, even his name. J.C.—Jared Cole or I miss my guess."

"You're wrong. It's Jared Charles."

"Liar. I could show you pictures of me about that age and you'd swear it was—" He sucked in a ragged breath, raking a hand through already disheveled hair. "Not that any of that matters. The minute I looked into his eyes, I knew."

"His eyes are brown," she declared, her voice shrill. "A lot of people have brown eyes." Not a lot of people had that gorgeous amber shade of brown, but perhaps he'd miss that point.

"I'm not talking about the color, I'm talking about the *connection*." He took a step toward her and his angry expression softened. "When I looked into his eyes, it was like a bolt of electricity passing through me." His mouth tilted cynically. "Much like the way I felt the first time I met his mother, in fact—that shock of recognition."

"Oh, Cole—" Jenny turned away.

He grabbed her shoulder and forced her to turn back toward him. "He's my son."

She lifted her chin. "He's not! He's *my* son. I had him alone, I've raised him alone—"

"By choice. What kind of woman would make a choice like that when it wasn't necessary?" He shook his dark head slowly. "What kind of woman are *you*, Jenny Wolf?"

"The kind you'll never understand—the kind who doesn't want anything from you except to be left alone!"

He reached out to slide the curving fingers of one hand around her neck, his thumb settling lightly but ominously on the indentation of her collarbone. His thoughts were very clear to her; *I could break your neck with one hand, and after the way you've deceived me—* She wouldn't flinch, she wouldn't!

Instead of tightening that grip, he took the single step that separated them and bent over her, his face mere inches from hers. When he spoke, she felt the warmth of his breath on her lips.

"I don't know whether to break your neck or pick you up and carry you off to bed," he grated. "I don't know which would bring me the most grief, so I guess I'd better do neither."

Only when he released her and stepped back did she realize she'd forgotten to breathe. Sucking in a great gasp of oxygen, she stared at him, as unsure as he about the consequences of the two choices he'd offered.

"Please—won't you just leave?" Through lips so stiff they hardly moved, she forced the words. "You're not welcome here, Cole. This is harassment, pure and simple. Go!"

"Yes, I'll go." He put his hand on the doorknob. "But only because I've got to think about all this. I feel as if I've just been through some kind of...some kind of earthquake. Considering what I've learned tonight, the big one in California pales by comparison."

"There's nothing to think about! J.C. isn't your son! You've got to believe that."

His sigh sounded tired. "Save your breath, Jenny. He's mine. He's mine, and tomorrow I'll tell you what I'm going to do about that."

"Do! But you can't—"

"Did you suppose I'd just walk away, once I knew?" His dark brows arched. "Of course you didn't, which is why you've worked so hard to keep me from finding out."

"That's not true. I—" She stopped, biting her lip. "He isn't yours Cole, he's mine. You don't know what you're saying."

"We both know what I'm saying." He opened the door, then hesitated. "And don't think you can grab him out of that bed and run. There's nowhere you can go, nowhere you can hide that I wouldn't find you. Save us all a lot of grief by behaving in a responsible manner, for once."

She stared at him, lips parted while she drew shallow, frightened gasps. This was her worst nightmare coming true, she realized.

He looked satisfied. "We'll talk tomorrow."

"No. I won't—"

"Yes, you will. I'm not asking you, I'm telling you. You've forfeited all right to an opinion by keeping the truth from me. I'll try to overlook that, since you seem to have done a decent job raising our son, but that's the past. His future is *mine*."

She stood there for a long time after the door had closed behind him. Her frantic thoughts plunged this way and that, looking for a loophole where none existed. Her first instinct was to run, but his warning had shown her the utter futility of that.

It took her all night to acknowledge that she had but one course open to her. She must brazen this out.

If she failed to convince him that J.C. wasn't his son, then she'd have to bargain with him...because if he decided to fight her for custody, she didn't think she'd have a chance.

She *had* lied to him, and American courts were bending over backward these days to be fair to fathers and protect their rights. Furthermore, he had wealth and power behind him, and what did she have besides an insupportable lie? She was a single working mother. Although she'd always put her son first, she was raising him in a tiny and isolated Rocky Mountain town while his father could offer him the world.

She arose exhausted the next morning. J.C. took one look at her and frowned.

"You sick, Mama?"

"No, no, I'm fine. But we'll have to hurry or we'll be late."

"Are you mad at me about something?"

She dropped to her knees and drew him into her arms, breathing in the little-boy scent and savoring the wiriness of the little-boy body. "Oh, no, I'm not mad at you at all! I love you, J.C. Wolf."

He kissed her cheek and she felt the smile on his lips. "I love you, too," he said. "Will your boss come see me again someday? I don't love him, but I like him pretty much."

The muscles of her stomach contracted painfully. "I . . . don't know. He's a very busy man, very important."

"Oh." J.C. looked disappointed. "He said he would, but sometimes grown-ups fib to kids."

She didn't think this grown-up had, to her grief. But she diverted the conversation away from Cole and finally managed to get both herself and her child ready to face the day.

She reported for work on the dot. Nona met her in the hall, eyes wide with curiosity.

"Mr. Stadler said to send you to his office the minute you arrive," his secretary said in a hushed whisper. "My goodness, Jenny, he looks like death warmed over—and now that I take a good look, you do, too. What in the world is going—?"

Jenny didn't wait for the rest of a question she couldn't answer. As her brother Jared always said, the best defense was a good offense.

She'd face Mr. Cole Stadler; she'd defy Mr. Cole Stadler.

And if that didn't work, she'd bargain with Mr. Cole Stadler. But under no circumstances would she let him take her son away from her.

He looked tired but also controlled, no raw edges of messy emotion showing anywhere.

While she—she must look like a stick of dynamite with a burning fuse. At least, that's how she felt walking into the lion's den. But if she had a prayer of winning, she must match his self-control. This was not the time to lose her head.

So she regarded him coolly, her chin in the air. "You wish to see me?" she murmured.

"That's right." He gestured to a leather-upholstered chair. "Please sit down."

"I prefer to stand."

He shrugged and tossed his pen on the desk blotter. "Suit yourself. But for what I have to say, you should be sitting."

Her blood ran cold. "What's that supposed to mean?"

"That I've decided on the best course of action."

All the oxygen seemed sucked from the room by his statement. She bit her trembling lip. He was going to try for custody, she just knew it. She forced herself to say coolly, "And that is . . . ?"

A slight smile curved his well-shaped mouth, but his eyes revealed no humor. "It's very simple, actually." He built a steeple with his fingertips. "I'm going to marry you, Jenny Wolf."

He knew that announcement would take the wind out of her sails, and it did. She sat down hard in the chair she'd refused moments earlier. What little color there had been in her cheeks washed away, leaving her pale and somehow distraught, although she didn't utter a sound.

He had never known a more beautiful woman than Jenny Wolf and she was more beautiful at this moment than she had ever been, more vulnerable. She was fighting for her life—for her child.

Well, so was he. There was nothing she could say that would convince him that the boy he'd met only a few hours ago wasn't his own flesh and blood, nothing that would sway him from his course. He did not seek to punish her for keeping his son from him, although he would do so if that's what it took.

She should be grateful for that, and for the fact that he'd decided marriage, not a custody battle, would be best for the boy. Custody fights could be brutal, not only for the parents but for the child. Now that he'd found J.C., he didn't intend to hurt him to have him.

But have him, he would. J.C. Wolf was about to become J.C. Stadler and no power on earth could change that outcome.

Certainly not the beautiful, faithless woman who leaned forward with one hand extended in supplication.

"That's insane! I'd never marry you!" It had taken her a few moments for his announcement to fully register, but now that it had she must overcome her shock and go on the offensive.

"Ah, Jenny, Jenny." He shook his head, a smile nudging his mouth. "There was a time you claimed you wanted nothing more than to spend your life with me."

"I was young then, and foolish."

"We were both foolish. But now we're older and presumably wiser. You must see that I intend to have my son."

She was shaking her head before he even finished. "But why this way? Marriage? That's crazy!"

"It's more expeditious than a custody battle."

She recoiled. *"He's not your son, Cole!"*

"Damn it!" He half rose from the desk chair, his amber eyes alight with fury. "Give up that fiction. He is my son."

"It's your word against mine. You can't prove—"

"Blood tests."

"B-blood—?"

"Blood tests can prove paternity. I'd hate to put him through that, but if you insist—"

She recoiled back in her chair, her eyelids closing out the sight of him, so confident and self-righteous. Well, how could she blame him? She'd played an awful trick on him . . . but only because he'd married someone else, she reminded herself. "I'll never marry a man who doesn't love me," she whispered, the words like arrows to her heart.

"Not even if that man is the father of your child, and loves that child every bit as much as you do? Not even if that man puts the welfare of that child above anything and everything on earth?"

She felt faint, beleaguered as she was by his measured arguments. "But a marriage in name only? He'd know—he'd sense that things weren't right."

The slow unveiling of his smile revealed an infinite capacity to hurt her. "Who says it would be in name only?" he inquired with soft malice.

"I'm going to marry you and it will be a real marriage with nothing held back—*nothing*. I want to make that very clear right from the beginning. And I'm talking about a lifetime, Jenny, make no mistake about that. Till death do us part..."

She bit back a groan. "Don't do this to me, Cole—don't do it to yourself! You'd condemn us both to a lifetime of misery just for revenge? I never meant to hurt you—"

"Or have my child, but it happened, didn't it?" He stood up restlessly. "You had no right to keep him from me."

"Even when I knew you'd married?"

"Yes, even then!" He threw back his shoulders and confronted her. "You took a coward's way out and now it's time to pay the piper."

"No, I can't." A lifetime with this bitter, vindictive man? She couldn't face that even in her worst nightmares. She didn't know what had happened to the Cole Stadler she'd loved, but she would not, could not share her life, her child—and certainly not her bed—with the man he'd become.

"All right," he said, seeming to draw back into himself.

She blinked. "A-all right?"

He nodded. "I can't force you. Hell, I *wouldn't* force you. You've got to be willing or we'll never be able to provide a proper homelife for J.C., and that's what this is all about." He reached the telephone and dialed.

"Who are you calling?" She stood, assuming she was being dismissed.

He arched one brow. "My lawyer. I'm starting legal action to take my son away from you. And since you're not willing to listen to reason, I'll settle for nothing less than full custody."

She couldn't believe she'd fainted, but the facts were incontrovertible. She regained her senses lying on his leather chaise longue, Cole seated beside her and chaffing her hands.

"W-what happened?" she murmured.

"You passed out before I could give you my final terms," he said.

She caught her breath and her heart began a steady drumming. "Terms?"

"You've got twenty-four hours."

"To do what?" She was so terribly confused she wasn't sure if he was talking about the custody fight or the marriage proposal.

"To make up your mind," he said. "J.C. deserves a family and we're going to give him one—or I'll do it alone, after I get custody. But in no case will things continue as they were."

She groaned and pressed the heels of her palms to her eyes.

"And to make sure you don't try anything funny," he continued relentlessly, "I'm not going to let you out of my sight until the decision is made."

For a few moments she lay there, feeling completely at his mercy. Then, with a superhuman effort, she sat up. "I'll never forgive you for this," she said in a ragged voice. "If I'd had any idea what kind of man you were, I'd never have let you get close to me on that accursed cruise!"

He looked at her, his smile sardonic. "Yes, you would," he said. "Because you couldn't help yourself...any more than you'll be able to help yourself now."

Through a long and hellish day, Jenny strove to regain her equilibrium. After a while, she thought if a single other person asked her what was wrong, she'd collapse into tears.

She saw Cole only at a distance, and even then she seemed to sense his faint and secret smile. He was so sure of himself, so certain of success.

But marriage? He must be out of his mind if he thought she'd let him force her into anything so drastic. She might still be the unsophisticated little mountain girl he'd...she hesitated, knowing that the proper word wasn't really *seduced* but unwilling to put any other name to what had happened between them. She did have resources, if she were willing to call upon them.

Her best resource was her brother Jared, who would support her in whatever she decided to do. But just thinking about Jared's temper—about his possessiveness—scared her. The last thing she wanted was to draw her brother into this mess.

Which would be the first thing that would happen, in a messy custody battle. She'd need Jared's moral support, but also his money. She certainly didn't have the financial means to fight the son and heir to a hotel empire alone.

What to do? At lunchtime, she managed to slip out a side door and spend the next hour wandering the byways of Cripple Creek, trying to avoid everyone she knew so she could think.

Think! Ever since Cole Stadler had come to town, she'd been trying to think, and where had it got her?

She'd no more than returned to work than the front door opened to admit her sister-in-law, Lark, with baby Gray in his pack on her back. She looked around anxiously, spotted Jenny and rushed forward.

"I've got to speak to you!" she hissed, looking around as if for eavesdroppers.

Jenny's heart plummeted. "Oh, my gosh, now what?"

Lark gestured toward the settee and two chairs arranged against a wall. "Over there, where we won't be overheard."

Jenny followed with an apologetic glance at her co-worker. Sinking onto a chair, she asked, "Are you all right? Is Jared—?"

"Fine, fine, we're all fine."

"Thank heavens. Then what is it, Lark?"

"I figured it out."

"You figured what out?"

"Please don't pretend with me, Jenny." Lark spoke primly. "About J.C."

"J.—" Jenny felt a hot flush wash over her cheeks.

Lark nodded. "You met Mr. Stadler when you went on that cruise all those years ago, am I right?"

"I—why, you—" Jenny stopped stumbling for words. She refused to lie to her brother's wife. Drawing a deep breath, she nodded miserably.

Lark sighed. "Then Cole Stadler really is J.C.'s father." Her eyes widened. "Jenny, is J.C.'s name really Jared *Cole*?"

Jenny opened her mouth to deny it but found herself unable to say the words. Dully she nodded.

Lark leaned forward to place her hand over Jenny's. "He didn't know he had a son until he saw J.C. last night, did he?"

Again, Jenny nodded, unsure why she felt so ashamed. "Nobody knew," she whispered. 'N-now that *you* do, I hope you won't...think less of me. There are...extenuating circumstances. I did what I thought I had to do."

"Oh, honey!" Lark's sympathy shone in her eyes. "I love you as if you really were my sister. Nothing will ever change that. But..."

"But what?"

Lark bit her lip, looking suddenly evasive. "But we've got another problem. I'm not the only one who's figured it out. Jared—"

Jenny jumped to her feet. "Jared! What did he say? What does he plan to do?"

"You mean before or after he kills the S.O.B. who seduced his little sister?" Lark, too, stood up, hoisting her baby backpack to a more comfortable position. "I dropped him off at your house to wait for you to come home from work. I told him I had a few errands to run and would meet him there later—but, oh, Jenny, I'm so worried!"

"How upset is he?"

"*Way* upset. I told him he needs the whole story before going off half cocked, but I don't know if I convinced him.'' She shook her head, giving Jenny an anxious glance. ''I think we'd better get right over there before Jared takes it into his head to come looking for you here—or for *him*.''

Jenny didn't need to ask which *him* Lark meant. If Jared and Cole met before she'd had a chance to soothe her brother, blood might very well flow again in the streets of Cripple Creek!

CHAPTER SEVEN

JENNY burst through the front door of her little house, her heart pounding with panic. She saw him at once—Jared, standing with his back toward the small stone fireplace on the opposite side of the room. His face was dark as a thundercloud.

She stopped short in the open doorway, suddenly uncertain how she should proceed. On the short drive up the mountain, she'd played one scenario after another over in her mind, finally deciding she had to at least *try* to brazen this out. But she'd expected Jared to be boiling with anger, not facing her with cold accusation in his eyes.

"J-Jared?" She licked her lips uncertainly. "I—"

"Hold on a minute," he said brusquely.

"Hold on—?"

"Yeah, what I have to say I want *him* to hear, too."

With a feeling of fresh dread, she realized he was looking past her, through the open doorway. Almost afraid of what she'd find, she turned to find Cole crossing the yard with long, determined strides.

"Oh, no," she moaned.

"Oh, yes!" Jared's tone was flat but filled with an anticipation that was almost scary.

Jenny clutched at her brother's elbow. "Please don't start anything," she begged. "It isn't what you think."

"It's exactly what I think." Jared wrapped an arm around her shoulders. "As your brother, it's my duty to protect you from guys like that."

"But you don't understand! There's nothing to protect me from. If you'll just—"

Cole stepped through the open doorway, his glance taking in brother and sister. "There you are, Jenny," he said easily. "I wondered why you took off so suddenly. I hope everything's all right."

"Everything's fine," she said quickly, giving Jared an anxious glance. "You didn't need to follow me."

"You knew I would." He spoke to her but his narrow gaze lifted to lock with Jared's. "Is J.C. all right?"

"Of course."

Jared made an angry, growling sound. "No thanks to you."

Cole tensed visibly. "What's that supposed to mean?"

"It means—" Jared set Jenny aside carefully. "It means I *know*. You're the bastard who seduced my sister while she was just a kid, seduced her and abandoned her without a thought—"

"That's a damned lie." Dark, angry color flooded Cole's lean cheeks.

Jared's mouth turned down contemptuously. "You deny you're J.C.'s father?"

"Deny it?" Cole's tawny eyes widened. "Hell, I'm proud of it!"

Jenny couldn't believe this. Clinging to her brother's arm, she glanced miserably from one man to the other. "Stop, both of you! Jared, Cole isn't— I mean, he didn't—"

Jared ignored her and spoke to Cole. "If you're proud of the boy, why did you let Jenny raise him all alone? Why weren't you providing for him all these years? For that matter, why didn't you do the right thing and marry his mother?"

"Because *I didn't know he existed*." Cole thrust his hands through his hair, the first indication of just how agitated he was. "For your further information, I didn't jilt your sister—she jilted me."

"That's not true!" Jenny cried. "Will the two of you stop talking about me as if I weren't even here? Cole is *not*—"

"Jenny!"

They said her name in unison, making her cringe before their mutual disbelief. Apparently neither would allow her to continue the fiction concerning J.C.'s paternity.

Cole continued relentlessly. "As soon as I found out, I proposed to her. She told me to take a hike, in so many words."

"Is that true?" Jared caught her by the upper arms and stared into her face. "Did he ask you to marry him?"

"Yes, but you don't understand." She was so agitated that she could barely speak. "He only did it because he wants to get his hands on J.C."

Cole laughed. "Not entirely. I want to get my hands on you, too."

"Don't even *think* about it until the ring's on her finger," Jared said grimly.

"And it never will be," Jenny inserted.

Jared frowned. "Why not? He wants to make an honest woman of you. Let him."

"No—never!"

"Why not?" Cole demanded.

"Yeah, Jen, why not?" Jared echoed.

"B-because—" Her lip trembled violently and she paused long enough to get control of it before blurting, "Oh, Cole, why did you have to come here? We were happy, J.C. and me. We don't need all this—this *confusion*!"

He studied her with brooding eyes. "I don't believe you were all that happy," he said finally. "I know for a fact that the boy misses having a father."

"That's the truth," Jared agreed. "You've said so yourself many a time, Jenny. Here's your chance to give him what should have been his all along."

"Jared, how could you!" She whirled on him in disbelief. "You're my brother. You're supposed to be on my side!"

"I am on your side," he argued. "All I want is what's best for you and your son. At this point, that appears to be Mr. Cole Stadler. The man wants to do the right thing—a little late—" He shot Cole a condemning glance. "But better late than never."

Cole dipped his head in acknowledgment. "I welcome your support," he said calmly.

Jenny couldn't believe what was happening. She'd thought of everything but this. "Jared—" She darted a helpless glance at Cole.

Jared understood. "Mind waiting outside while I have a little word with my sister?" he said to Cole, voice suddenly mild.

"Not at all." Cole backed toward the door. "I'll be right outside, but I warn you, I'm not a patient man."

The door closed behind him. Tears burned the backs of Jenny's eyelids. "Don't do this to me, Jared," she begged in a husky voice. "Please don't."

"Do what, Jen?" He gave her a glance that might have been mostly pity. "Urge you to marry the man you love?"

"But I don't—" Indignant, she turned away. "What makes you think—"

"I know you." He stepped up behind her and slid his arms around her shoulders in a fond embrace. "You loved him once or you'd never have slept with him on that blasted cruise, am I right?"

She let her breath out on a long mournful note. She couldn't lie about that. "Okay, I loved him once. But that was a long time ago. Everything's different now."

"Not so very different. You've lived alone all these years, which tells me you still love him."

"No!" She shook her head violently. "That's not true."

"Oh? Then why?"

"Well, I— It's just that I've never met— I've been too busy raising my son—" She stumbled to a halt, knowing she sounded defensive.

"His son, too."

Jenny twisted around until she could face him. "That's all he really wants, you know—J.C."

"Not *all*. But even if it was, who could blame him? Any man worth his salt would want his son. That was a terrible thing you did, Jenny, not telling him."

"I had my reasons." Reasons she didn't want to explain to anyone at this point. "But I won't marry him."

"Why not?"

"Because . . . living with and loving a man who doesn't love me back would kill me." As it almost killed her to admit to such a thing.

Jared smiled, cupping her cheek with one hand. "I don't buy that for a minute, baby sister. Any man in his right mind would love you—hell, maybe he already does."

She shook her head stubbornly. "I can't take that chance. What if he got his hands on J.C. and then decided to cut me out of the picture? Then I really *would* die."

"No, you wouldn't." Jared dropped a quick kiss on her forehead. "Because to get to you, he'd have to go through me." Straightening, he called brusquely, "You still out there, Stadler?"

The front door opened so promptly that Jenny had to wonder if he'd been standing with his ear pressed to it.

Cole stepped inside. "What's the law about wedding licenses in this state?" he asked.

Jenny gasped. "Why do you want to know? There's no way I'll—"

Jared cut her off. "No waiting period, no blood test. You can get a license over at the courthouse on West Bennett. It'll cost you twenty dollars cash money and it's good for thirty days."

Cole grinned. "You sound pretty up-to-date on the subject."

Jared grinned back. "I got married myself, not so very long ago. So what do you say, sis?"

"About what?" Why did she have this incredulous feeling that they were engaging in a conspiracy against her?

"About getting a marriage license," Cole said patiently.

"Why bother?" She lifted her chin. "It would never be used. You'd just be out your twenty bucks."

"I can afford it." Cole smiled. "In case you changed your mind, we'd have it ready."

"I won't change my mind."

"Want to bet?"

She backed away from both of them, feeling completely overwhelmed. "I've had enough of this nonsense. Will you both please just *go*?"

"Can't," Jared said. "Lark's got the car. I'm afoot."

"I'm sure Cole wouldn't mind giving you a ride." She was instantly sorry for suggesting it; they were already conspiring against her.

Cole didn't give her a chance to take it back. "Not at all." He gestured for Jared to proceed him through the doorway.

She watched them walk across the yard together, shoulder to shoulder, talking as intently as if they were old friends.

Her brother, her very own brother, had betrayed her. She could hardly believe it.

Cole returned later that same evening, just as she prepared to tuck J.C. into bed. When the boy saw who stood on the front porch, he leapt across the room in his pajamas and threw himself into the man's arms.

"Did you come to read me a story?" he demanded. "Will you tuck me in bed?"

"Yes and yes." Cole swung the boy into the air before setting him on his feet. "I'm sure your mother won't mind."

She minded very much, but felt powerless to protest. She wouldn't leave them alone, however.

Thus she saw J.C. kiss this interloper's cheek, heard her son whisper, "Good night, I love you," in someone else's ear. By the time tucking chores were complete, she was not only nervous but depressed.

Once back in the living room, she refused to look at him. "I hope you don't think you can make a habit of that," she said.

"Of what? Tucking my son into—"

"Don't! Don't call him that! He might hear." She cast a frightened glance toward the hallway.

"That's something we have to talk about."

"I don't want to talk to you about *anything*. Just go—please."

"We've got to talk, Jenny." He led her to the couch and pressed her into the cushions, sitting beside her. His tawny gaze was intense. "I want to tell him who I am."

The bottom dropped out of her stomach. "No!"

"Yes. He has to know sooner or later—hell, he has a right to know."

"Not now, not now. It would be devastating—" Yes, devastating for J.C. to know he had a father and then to lose that father again—and he would. Jenny still intended to leave Cripple Creek. Of course, now it would be harder; Jared would probably refuse to lend her any money. If he did, she'd still find a way; she *had* to, even if it meant selling the diamond.

Frustration crossed Cole's face. "I don't know how much more of this I can handle, Jenny. Every minute I'm with him, the words hang there in the back of my throat—*I'm your father. You're my son. I love you.*"

"If you love him, you'll give me—give *him* time to adjust to all this. He hardly even knows you. Please, Cole, promise me you won't say anything until I'm sure the time is right."

"Will you ever be sure?"

"I— Yes, of course." She prayed she didn't sound evasive. "I'll know when the time is right."

He looked at her as if he were trying to decide whether or not to believe her. Suddenly those golden eyes began to gleam. "Let's make a deal," he said.

Something told her she wasn't going to like this. "What kind of deal?"

"If you'll come with me to get a marriage license, I'll hold off telling him...for a while, anyway."

She stared at him. "That's blackmail!"

"You think so?" He smiled. "Lighten up, Jenny. Just because we get a license doesn't mean we have to use it. What do you say? Deal?"

He was crowding her ever closer to what he wanted, without regard for her feelings. Yet, what bargaining power did she have? She'd never marry him but if he wanted to throw away twenty dollars— "I'll have to think about it," she said at last.

He nodded, his eyelids drifting down until they half covered those remarkable eyes. "All right. While you're thinking about it, think about this, too—"

Catching her by the shoulders, he lifted her to meet his descending lips in a kiss that burned all the way down to the pit of her stomach. Just as quickly, he set her aside and stood up.

"Happy dreams," he murmured. "I'll see you tomorrow at work."

"T-tomorrow," she agreed, wanting to touch her tingling mouth with the tips of her fingers, knowing that until he was out of the room she didn't dare give in to temptation.

Cole seemed determined to spend every spare moment with J.C., which meant Jenny was subjected to his company practically every waking hour, counting her time at work. She had to admit, though, that he was wonderful with the boy. It wasn't too difficult for Cole to coax her into letting J.C. go into town for ice cream, on a drive into the mountains, to play catch in the front yard. The man always managed to bring up these things in the boy's presence, which made it almost impossible for his mother to say no.

Where J.C. went, Jenny also went, albeit reluctantly. J.C. and Cole were growing closer and closer right before her eyes. In a panic, she spent every spare moment trying to figure a way out of this mess, which meant a way out of Cripple Creek. No immediate solution presented itself.

And always, Cole pushed her. A week following his ultimatum—the one he called a proposal—he confronted her after J.C. was in bed for the night.

"Your week's up," he announced. "Are you going to marry me or what?"

"Or what," she said tartly, although her heart plummeted. She'd hoped he'd . . . what? Change his mind? Forget the time limit he'd set? Fat chance!

His expression altered in some subtle way, becoming harder and more relentless. "Then I'll tell him I'm his father tomorrow morning. I'll be here when he gets up and—"

"No, Cole. No!" She faced him defiantly. "I can't let you hurt him that way."

"Hurt him? Hurt him! You're the one who—" He broke off his impassioned words and sucked in a deep breath. "I promised myself I wouldn't start throwing blame around and I won't. But know this, Jennifer Wolf. I am that boy's father and I will have a father's role in his life—one way or another."

She gasped. "Is that a threat?"

"No, sweetheart." He slipped one hand around her neck and pulled her forward. "That's a promise."

His mouth came down on hers, hot and hard and demanding. She tasted anger in his kiss and something else, as well, something that sent a shiver of longing all the way down to her toes. When he lifted his head, he was breathing hard.

"Think about it," he whispered. "All you have to do is go with me to get the license—but it's got to be tomorrow. No more stalling, Jenny."

It was difficult for her to reply when he held her so close, when she could see the silky fan of his lashes and lose her equilibrium in the amber depths of his eyes. It took superhuman effort to defy him. "A license is just a piece of paper. If I agree—"

She couldn't miss the flare of triumph in his eyes. "*If I agree*, it still wouldn't mean I'll marry you."

"Maybe not, but it's one step closer—for marry me, you will."

He buried his face in the curve of her shoulder, surprising her, making her tremble at the feel of his cheek pressed beneath her chin. Her hands fluttered up and she caught herself just in time to prevent herself from caressing his back, from melting into his embrace.

His voice was a muffled murmur. "No, damn it, your brother's right—not until the ring's on your finger." He straightened and stepped away, releasing her abruptly. "I'd better leave while I still can," he said. "Good night, Jenny Wolf."

The parting kiss he dropped on her cheek was almost . . . innocent.

"Marry the guy, Jenny."

"Oh, Jared, leave her alone, why don't you?" Lark gave Jenny a compassionate glance. "Can't you give the poor girl a little breathing room?"

"She's had five years' worth of breathing room," Jared said relentlessly. "What's holding you up, Jen? Even Lark—"

"What?" Jenny looked accusingly at her sister-in-law. "Even Lark what?"

"Likes him," Jared said.

Jenny couldn't believe it. "You don't even know him, Lark."

Lark looked uncomfortable. "Well, actually I do...a little. I had coffee with him the other day. I must say, he does seem to have J.C.'s best interests at heart."

Jenny's stomach clenched painfully. Cole was winning over all her former allies, one by one. If he could so easily convert her own family, how long would it take him to twist a judge around his little finger?

"I can't talk about this now," she said in a voice that trembled.

"Oh, Jenny, I'm sorry if that sounded disloyal—"

"Please, my break's over. I've got to get back to work."

"But—"

"I'll see you soon." She kissed Gray's soft baby cheek and jumped out of the frying pan and into the fire; Cole was waiting for her at the front desk.

"I'd like to speak to you in my office, Jenny," he said with calm certainty.

"But I'm just getting back from my coffee break. I'm sure Faith needs my help—"

"Oh, no, everything's fine," Faith said. "You run along."

So there was nothing left for Jenny to do but follow him into his office and brace herself for a showdown.

She sat in the leather chair before his desk, hands folded sedately in her lap. Inside, she felt anything but sedate. He would try to bully her, she felt sure; try to force her to do something completely against her will.

"Jenny," he began slowly, almost painfully, "it's time—"

"Stop right there, Cole Stadler." Jenny tried to speak with authority. "I know why you've brought me in here and I warn you, it's not going to work. I won't be treated this way, do you hear me? You're not going to blackmail me, or trick me, or con me or—" She paused, frowning. "Why are you looking at me that way?"

The way he was looking at her was with a kind of melancholy sadness, almost as if he disliked what he planned to say as much as she would dislike hearing it. He sighed. "Because I don't like talking about my marriage, but under the circumstances, I think you have a right to know. It might help you to make up your mind."

She was too stunned to disagree.

* * *

"Lynette was the girl next door. Her parents and mine were the best of friends and no one ever doubted that eventually the two families would be joined by our marriage."

Jenny listened to every painful word, not sure if the pain was his or hers or equally divided. "You loved her," she said, and knew who suffered from *those* words.

"Yeah, I guess so, sure." His face was haggard; he didn't look as if he'd slept much last night. "Not the way I loved you—completely different, as a matter of fact. When I saw you on that cruise ship—" He broke off and shook his head. "But that's a different story. Yes, I loved her and she loved me. She also counted on me, depended on me, took me for granted in a lot of ways. And I let her."

He leaned forward, resting his forearms on the desktop. "I returned from that cruise completely infatuated with you and determined to break it off with her. I told my parents—"

"Your parents!"

He shrugged. "I needed them to understand, perhaps help me cushion the blow to Lynette and her family. My mother and father... seemed to understand."

Jenny just bet they did: that their son had been taken in by some tramp on a cruise ship—

"All they asked was that I be sure of my feelings before doing anything irrevocable. I promised I'd talk to you one more time before I told Lynette—but you never called."

"I told you why."

"I don't *care* why, not anymore." His voice cracked like a whip. "The reason didn't matter much. The wedding went forward and I let it, after it became painfully apparent that I wasn't going to hear from you anyway. Lynette and I were married, we went on our honeymoon, we came back and went on with our lives."

"I...did call," she reminded him. "I don't suppose she told you about that."

His laughter was harsh. "As a matter of fact, I believe she did. She said I'd got a call from *some woman* who didn't leave a message. My heart stopped beating—I was sure it was you but there wasn't a damned thing I could do about it."

"She really told you?"

"Lynette didn't have a jealous bone in her body. She was completely sure of me. After...you, there was no reason for her to doubt me."

"I see." But it would take a while to understand.

"Our son was born about a year later." The words were coming harder and harder to him; his facial muscles tight with the effort. "We loved him—adored him. Everyone said what a handsome baby he was, how bright and happy. He looked a lot like—" He stopped, his expression stricken. "He made everything worthwhile—and then he and his mother were gone."

Cole brushed one hand across his eyes as if sweeping away the cobwebs of a past too painful to relive. Jenny sat with one clenched fist pressed beneath her rib cage, anything to help her control the grief his words conjured up.

"It was a fire," Cole went on relentlessly. "And because I hadn't really loved Lynette as I should, I had guilt to struggle with, as well as grief. I decided then and there that I'd never expose myself to that kind of pain again."

His glance condemned her. "If I hadn't discovered J.C., I never would have. But you took choice away from me—he's already here, he's mine and I love him." His sharp gaze bored into her. "What happens next is up to you, Jenny."

Was it? Was it really? *She* had no real choices, either. She no longer had the resources to run away from her problems, which she now acknowledged would hardly have been a solution anyway. She hadn't realized the depth of Cole's determination. He would have found them, no matter where they'd gone.

So she surrendered. "All right, Cole. You win. We'll get the marriage license if that will satisfy you, but that's as far as it goes—that and my promise that when the time is right, we'll tell J.C. together—"

But he was shaking his head vigorously, finally interrupting the flow of her words. "That's no longer good enough," he said. "Marriage is—"

"No! I've told you what I'm willing to do."

"Now I'll tell *you* what *I'm* willing to do. The only way I can be reasonably sure you won't take off with my son is to marry you. If you still refuse, I will insist—legally and every other way— on being acknowledged as J.C.'s father. He'll be Jared Cole Stadler."

"No, you can't do that!"

"Yes, I can," he said softly. "And I can also demand—not ask, not insist, *demand*—custody. Your call, Jenny—marriage or the fight of your life. What'll it be?"

CHAPTER EIGHT

"YOU win, Cole." Jenny had never felt more helpless than when she said those words. It was over; she'd lost and she knew it at last. "If marriage is the only way to avoid—"

"It is!" The light of triumph leapt into his tawny eyes.

"For our son's sake," she added, bitterness seeping into her voice.

He shrugged, as if that were too obvious to deserve further comment. He looked like a different man, the pain of the past moments swept away by her capitulation, however reluctantly won. "Here's the plan, Jenny. The ceremony will be next Saturday—"

"So soon!" She braced tense forearms on the chair rests, feeling cornered. "Why not just get the license and see how everything goes? Jared said it was good for thirty days."

He shook his head forcefully. "We're past that. I'll arrange the ceremony for Saturday at 4:00 p.m. in the bridal suite upstairs. I'll be there with a minister and witnesses—and you'll be there, too, unless you want to start a war you can't possibly win."

"Saturday's too soon!" Gripping the armrests tightly, she half rose.

"No, Jenny." He came around the desk, lifting her the rest of the way and standing her on her feet. "It's too late—five years too late."

She couldn't look at him. "But I need time."

"What for? It's settled—and don't even *think* about running away."

"You mean, don't think about running away with *your son*. It would probably serve your purposes very well if I'd just take off alone, never to be heard from again. Well, I won't!" She brought fisted hands down on his chest for emphasis. "He's my son, too. I'll never give him up. Everything I've ever done, I've done for him."

For a moment he looked into her face, his expression strangely remote. "I repeat," he said, "don't even *think* about running away." Slipping an arm possessively around her waist, he turned her toward the door. "Now let's go announce our engagement and get that marriage certificate."

"Announce our—" She tried to hold back but it was like resisting the force of a tornado: an exercise in futility. This situation, like her life, was completely out of control.

Cole called together all the employees who could leave their posts of duty and made the big announcement in the private hotel lounge. To Jenny's consternation, no one seemed the least bit surprised.

If only she were as good an actress as he was an actor, she thought, standing uncomfortably by his side to accept hearty congratulations.

Taken on face value, you'd have thought him the happiest man on earth.

Nona, teary-eyed and beaming, kissed Jenny's cheek. "I'm so happy for you, honey," she declared. "When's the big day?"

Jenny darted a skittish glance at the man beside her. "We've not actually—"

"Saturday," Cole cut in. He tightened his grip on her waist. "Saturday at four in my suite. It'll be a small, family affair, followed by a reception in the hotel ballroom—and you're all invited to that, right, sweetheart?"

He dropped a light kiss on the top of Jenny's head and she found herself forced to agree with him yet again.

When all the well-wishers had filed out, he turned to her with barely concealed eagerness. "Let's go tell J.C.," he said.

"Tell him what?"

"That we're getting married, of course."

Relief sliced through her; she'd thought he'd meant to tell J.C. of his paternity. But still she hesitated. "Not yet," she pleaded. "Let me get used to the idea first."

He didn't look happy. "Okay," he finally agreed. "We can tell him after we get the license, I suppose."

She drew a deep, determined breath and nodded. "How about picking up the license Friday? There's no hurry, after all."

He burst out laughing. Hands on her waist, he picked her up and whirled her around the empty lounge until she was breathless and clinging to him. When he set her on her feet, she hung on to him dizzily.

He grinned down at her. "You make me fight and bargain for every inch you give me," he said, but cheerfully. "Why don't you just relax and let it happen, Jenny? You know it will. We're going to get the license and get married and tell J.C. who I really am. And then...and then, my beautiful bride-to-be, we're going to spend our wedding night right here in the bridal suite— finally put old Able the ghost out of his misery. All this is as inevitable as sunrise and tides." He brushed a thumb over her full lower lip. "I've found you and you'll never get away from me again...and that, also, was inevitable."

Before she could protest, he kissed her, bending her back over the arm clamped around her waist. Dizzy and disoriented, she could only cling to him and wonder how she was going to survive, pitted against this force of nature.

They went straight to the courthouse for the marriage license, which was a snap; telling J.C. proved to be a bit more difficult, at least for Jenny. Cole insisted on driving her to the baby-sitter's to pick the boy up, and then to her little house on the hill. He seemed determined not to let her spend a moment more than necessary out of his sight, and she supposed she couldn't blame him, under the circumstances.

At her cottage, Cole and J.C. played catch in the front yard while Jenny threw together a quick supper of grilled cheese sandwiches and mugs of tomato soup. It wasn't much; actually, she wasn't a bad cook, under the right circumstances. But if Cole thought she was going to slave over a hot stove on his behalf—

She pulled herself up short, holding a spatula poised to flip the sandwiches. What was she thinking of? He wasn't after a cook; he *hired* cooks. Nor did he need a housekeeper or a secretary or any such thing. He wanted his son, first and foremost, and then, apparently, someone to warm his bed . . . but not his heart.

How had she gotten herself into such a mess? His revenge would be even more total if she let him see how much she cared for him.

Brushing away tears, she flipped the sandwiches before crossing to the window to call the ballplayers in to eat. One thing she'd never do was let him see her cry.

"Can I have that last sandwich, Mama?" J.C. eyed the remaining golden triangle on the serving plate.

"*May* I have the last sandwich—and of course you can." She pushed the plate toward him with a smile, thinking that as long as he ate she'd be able to avoid the moment of truth.

He reached for it, then hesitated to glance at Cole. "Wanna share, Mr. Stadler?"

Cole shook his head. "You go ahead, sport." He watched the boy take a big bite before adding in a casual tone, "J.C., there's something your mother and I would like to tell you."

"Yeah?" The boy looked up, his amber eyes bright but not apprehensive.

"Not yet," Jenny said hastily. "After dessert. I've got chocolate ice cream—"

"This is better than chocolate ice cream," Cole said firmly.

J.C. laughed incredulously. "Hardly nothin's that good," he said.

"This is," Cole promised. He smiled at Jenny, then at the boy. "Your mother and I are getting married."

"Married?" J.C. frowned without understanding.

Cole nodded. "Do you know what that means?"

The boy cocked his head, wrinkling his forehead in thought. "What?" he finally asked.

Jenny held her breath while Cole leaned forward, his hands on the table.

"It means we'll be a family," he said softly. "A little boy, a mother...and a father. Would you like that, J.C.?"

"You mean like...a daddy?"

J.C. didn't look ready to believe it. His skepticism tore at Jenny's heart. "That's right, sweetheart," she assured him. "Mr. Stadler wants to be your daddy, but if you don't like the idea—" She shot a challenging glance at the man who'd gone completely still in his seat at the small dinette table.

As one, Jenny and Cole held their breath, waiting for one five-year-old child to decide all their fates. For a long time, the boy sat there, frowning thoughtfully. Then he looked up with a grin.

"I guess it's okay," he said. "Do you know how to be a daddy, Mr. Stadler?"

That innocent remark must hurt terribly under the circumstances, Jenny thought, but Cole didn't let on that he'd loved and lost another little boy. He just smiled at J.C.

"I've had a little bit of experience, and I'm a fast learner," he said. "Maybe you'll help me."

"Sure." J.C. nodded, then added in a dreamy voice, "I always wanted a daddy. Yeah, that'd be cool, I guess." He grinned suddenly. "Way cool, Mr.—should I call you Daddy or what?"

Jenny couldn't tell if the tears were in her eyes or Cole's. Later, she told him haltingly how much she appreciated his restraint in not telling J.C. the entire truth.

"He was up to it but I'd about hit my limit," Cole admitted. "But he has to know soon, Jenny—real soon."

Jared and Lark had to be told, of course. The next afternoon—Tuesday, only four days before the wedding—Cole drove J.C. and Jenny up the mountain in his BMW. It was a beautiful summer day, the air clear as crystal and sweet as the new-mown hay in Jared's fields. Jenny watched the familiar landscape with a feeling of unreality.

She still wasn't reconciled to this, couldn't believe it would happen. Or maybe didn't *want* to believe it. Cole, on the other hand, seemed perfectly comfortable with the situation.

"Which way?"

Startled from her thoughts, Jenny glanced up to see a fork ahead in the two-lane mountain road. "To the left," she instructed automatically.

"Where does the other road lead?" he asked curiously.

"To an old log cabin built more than a century ago by my Indian ancestors."

"No kidding." He took the left fork. "Does it still belong to your family?"

"Yes."

"Do you ever go there?"

"I haven't been there in a couple of years. Jared takes care of it, considers it a sort of family treasure because it's all handmade—" As she talked, she realized Cole seemed really interested in this bit of Wolf family history. Probably an act, she thought tiredly.

From the back seat, J.C. called out, "Hey, we're almost there!"

And they were. The car crested a pine-covered ridge and the Wolf family ranch lay before them.

Lark and Jared came out to meet them before the car had rolled to a stop on the curved gravel driveway in front of the house. They'd no more than disembarked when J.C. shouted out the news.

"Hey, Uncle Jared, I'm gonna get a new daddy!"

Lark and Jared exchanged quick glances, then turned to shower Jenny and Cole with hugs and congratulations. But as soon as everything quieted down, as soon as J.C. had rushed off to see the pony in the log corral next to the barn, as soon as Jared had led Cole away to see the new computer system where all the ranch records were kept, Lark's concerns spilled out.

"Are you sure this is what you want, honey?" she asked anxiously. "I know it's what *he* wants, and Jared's all in favor, and even J.C.—J.C. doesn't *know*, does he?"

"Not yet."

Lark nodded. "I thought not. So what about you? You don't seem . . . forget happy. I have the impression you're not even reconciled to this marriage."

"Everything will be fine," Jenny murmured, turning away. "Look, the aspens are beginning to turn—"

"Forget the aspens." Lark blocked Jenny's path. "It's *you* I'm worried about. If there's anything I can do to help . . ."

Jenny meant to keep a stiff upper lip, meant to smile and change the subject. But the caring on Lark's face undid her and the words she'd vowed not to say came tumbling out.

"I didn't have any choice—it still doesn't feel real. He wants his son and that's the beginning and the end of it. Either I marry him or face a custody fight I doubt I could ever win."

"Good grief!" Lark stared at her sister-in-law with wide eyes. "But the way he looks at you— I can't believe he intends this to be some . . . you know, some phony in-name-only sort of marriage."

"He *doesn't* intend that, which makes it even worse. He's made it perfectly clear—" Jenny stopped, biting her lip, her head drooping. She felt Lark's arm, warmly reassuring, on her shoulders.

"You really love him, don't you?"

"No!" Jenny jerked away, trembling. "How could I love him? He's come in here and disrupted my life, forced me to say and do things I'd never have said or done on my own, threatened to take my son away from me—no, I don't...yes... Oh, Lark, yes! It's true. I love him and I hate him and he's got so much power over me that it scares me to death."

"Now, now." Lark gentled Jenny with a hug, then led her toward the broad veranda running along the front of the house. "The only power he has over you is what you choose to give him."

"You don't understand!"

"I *do* understand. I fell in love once myself, remember?"

"Yes, but that was with Jared." Jenny glanced toward the barn just in time to see the two men disappear inside. "Jared's a pussycat, and he loved you back. It's not the same at all."

Lark laughed incredulously. "You sure have a selective memory! Have you forgotten that I was engaged to another man when Jared and I met again in the old family cabin after all those years? And that he hated, absolutely hated, my father and blamed him for every bad thing that ever happened in your family?"

"Well, yes, but—"

"But nothing, Jenny. You know what they say—the road to true love never runs smooth. If you love Cole, marry him and try to make something out of it. If you don't love him...well, you know your brother and I will back you in whatever you decide, our own feelings aside."

Jenny could barely bring herself to ask, "And your feelings are . . . ?"

Lark sighed. "Jared likes him, as I said, which is a total shock to me. I didn't think he'd ever admit anyone was good enough for his sister, especially the man who—well, you know."

"What about you?"

"I like him, too," Lark admitted. "I think he's a good man who obviously loves his son . . . and I wouldn't be at all surprised if he loved his son's mother, too. One thing I feel very strongly, however."

"And that is?"

"He'll never hurt you, Jenny, not on purpose, anyway. Like your brother, he'll make mistakes. Maybe the two of you won't see eye to eye on everything—"

"*Any*thing!"

Lark smiled. "Be that as it may, I can't believe he'll ever deliberately hurt you."

She led Jenny to the front door and opened the screen. "At least that's what I think, but what you think is more important. Just remember, we're here for you if you need us. Okay?"

"Okay." Jenny followed her sister-in-law into the house, wondering why that failed to reassure her.

At work the next day—Wednesday—Jenny found a single red rose in a bud vase waiting for her when she took her position behind the registration desk. She read his card: *Two days and counting*.

"Isn't that sweet?" Cole's secretary murmured in the bride-to-be's ear. "He just can't do enough for you, dear. You're such a lucky girl!"

He just can't do enough *to* me, Jenny thought with a pang of foreboding. Was he worried that she might yet pick up and run for her life? As if there were a chance of that happening...

Still, she knew he must half expect her to disappear as she had from the cruise ship. But it was too late for that...wasn't it? The die was cast; she couldn't escape her fate.

She thought she'd resigned herself until he took her on a tour of the bridal suite on Thursday. She'd gone reluctantly, only to be enchanted with what she saw. Workmen and decorators had been busy; she couldn't believe they'd turned the half-renovated apartment into a sunny bower filled with antiques and Victorian touches.

Standing on one side of the beautifully carved four-poster bed, she stared down at the lacy white coverlet with its profusion of pillows. Matching bed curtains looped to form a backdrop, restrained by opulent golden cords.

She'd never seen anything more lovely, more perfect for— She felt the blood drain from her face. Slowly she raised her head, her gaze locking with Cole's, standing opposite her across the bed.

He smiled. "Does it meet your expectations for your wedding night?" he asked softly. "Is there anything you'd like me to change, to add or subtract?"

Subtract me, she thought, but saw no point in saying it out loud. "It's...lovely."

He frowned. "Damning with faint praise? Come on, Jenny, you can't dread our honeymoon all *that* much. As I recall—"

"Don't remind me." She turned quickly away. "Then, I went to you of my own free will. This time—" She swallowed hard.

"This time will be of your own free will, too."

"How long are you prepared to wait?" she asked with thinly veiled sarcasm.

She heard him approach, felt the weight of his hands like shackles on her shoulders.

"I won't have to wait. Don't kid yourself, Jenny, our physical relationship will never be a problem." He lifted her heavy hair and kissed the curve of her neck, sending a jolt of electricity down her spine. "You want me, sweetheart." He bracketed her hips with his hands and nibbled at her ear. "I could have you on that bed in five minutes."

He turned her in his arms and his hot gaze mesmerized her. It was true; she was powerless to resist him.

He gave her an almost painful smile and added, "But I won't. As much as I want to make love to you, I'm going to wait. Day after tomorrow, the waiting will be over. Then it'll just be you and me and our son, the way it always should have been."

There seemed nothing she could say to that.

Agonizing doubts continued to plague her. Every time she looked at J.C., she was reminded of all Cole had already lost: a beloved son, a beloved wife. How could she think about keeping another son from him, even if she could find a way that offered reasonable hopes of success?

But as the minutes sped past at a dizzy rate on Saturday, her wedding day, she suddenly realized that she had to try. Looking at the simple Victorian summer dress she'd chosen in lieu of a wedding gown, she felt sick with anxiety.

Justify it as he might try, she was still being forced into this—and she'd had enough. If she had to sell the diamond ring to finance an escape, she would.

Was this why she'd rejected Lark's eager offer to help her dress for her wedding? Jenny wondered. Had she known all along that when push came to shove, she wouldn't be able to go through with it?

Rushing to her closet, she reached up on the top shelf and hauled down her largest suitcase, the same suitcase she'd taken on that ill-fated cruise. Throwing clothing willy-nilly into the bag, she called to J.C.

"Honey, could you come in here a minute? There's something I have to tell you."

"Mama?" The boy appeared in the doorway, a half-puzzled, half-frightened expression on his face. "What's the matter?"

"Nothing." She tried to smile, failed. "Come here, sweetheart."

He crossed the small room to stand before her, his eyes wide. Sitting on the edge of her bed, she pulled him into her arms. Holding him there, she could feel the rapid beating of his heart, the way his hands clutched at her.

She had to get hold of herself, for his sake. Swallowing hard, she pulled back enough to allow her to see his face.

"Mama, why are you crying?"

He reached out a grubby hand to touch tears she didn't know were falling, such compassion on his face that it made her want to weep in earnest.

"Because... honey, I don't think I can marry Mr. Stadler today."

He blinked, long curling lashes sweeping his tanned cheekbones. "Why not?"

A reasonable question, under ordinary circumstances. "B-because... I'm not sure it's the right thing to do."

J.C. just looked at her as if waiting for her to make her point. At last he said, "Doesn't he want to be my daddy anymore?"

His question broke her heart. "Of course he does! But there's more to it than that, darling. We'd have to live together, all of us. He'd have to be my... husband, and I'm not sure—no, I am sure. I don't want a husband." She busied herself smoothing his T-shirt, brushing back his tousled hair, anything to keep from examining his expression too closely.

He just stood there, quietly waiting.

She licked her lips. "I was... uh... thinking we might... go away somewhere."

"Just you and me?"

She rubbed her thumbnail over a spot of dried mud on his sleeve. "Yes. Do you think that would be all right?'' Still without looking at his face, she pulled him back into her arms. She felt his slight body shudder.

"Da—Mr. Stadler said he loves me," the boy whispered.

She closed her eyes, continuing to stroke the back of his head. "I'm sure he does. But he doesn't love me, sweetheart, and to make a family—"

"Oh, he does! He said so!"

"You must have misunderstood," she said gently, speaking around a knot in her chest that wouldn't go away. "It just wouldn't work, sweetheart. That's why I think we should go away, just you and me. We can go right now—what do you say?"

"Okay, Mama." Slowly J.C. straightened. "I don't need a daddy anyway." Tears rolled down his brown cheeks and he added a strangled, "Much..."

CHAPTER NINE

FOUR o'clock came and went, and still no Jenny.

Cole stood at the window in the bridal suite of the Miner's Repose Hotel with his back to the small assemblage, looking down on the hustle and bustle on the street below. Cripple Creek was swarming with tourists, some come to gamble and some just to soak up the Wild West atmosphere, but all in a holiday mood.

Cole was definitely *not* in a holiday mood.

He'd planned everything so carefully. The suite in which he stood had been decorated exactly as he'd instructed, with garlands of apricot roses looped before the fireplace, cold in summer's warmth. The round table near the window held a large silver bowl filled with bottles of champagne, and lovely silver-and-crystal plates of perfect luscious strawberries and mounds of whipped cream.

Beyond the inner door, he'd ordered that the bed be covered with a blanket of fragrant rose petals, and great bouquets of roses banked around the room. Those arrangements would be carried out as soon as the ceremony was complete and they'd all left to attend the reception below in the ballroom.

If the ceremony ever was complete... He clenched his teeth together in frustration.

She wasn't coming.

Now he'd have to track her down and drag her back—or worse, involve lawyers and the courts. Legal proceedings could only hurt them all, but especially the boy Cole sought to protect...the boy he was determined to claim as his own.

"Are you all right, son?"

At the sound of his mother's anxious voice, Cole turned with a quick smile. John and Laura Stadler had dropped everything to rush here from California for the wedding of their only son. How he'd longed to tell them that they had a grandson when he'd called to break the news. Instead, he'd simply asked them to support his seemingly irrational decision to marry a woman they naturally believed he'd met only a few weeks ago.

And they *had* supported him. Looking into his mother's concerned face, then his father's, Cole felt a surge of love and gratitude toward his parents. He'd taken them for granted, he realized, but that was about to change.

"I'm fine," he said gruffly, a not-quite-honest answer to his mother's soft question. "Once you get to know Jenny—" *If* you get to know Jenny. "You'll realize that being late for her own wedding is strictly in character."

His mother smiled uncertainly but seemed willing to take the explanation at face value. John Stadler's narrow gaze met his son's and he nodded. They were a handsome couple, Cole thought with pride. John was only an inch or two less than his son's six-foot-one, and he carried himself with complete assurance. Cole's mother had been acknowledged as quite a beauty in her day, and even in her fifties she retained the pale, flawless skin and glorious amber eyes.

John slipped an arm about her waist. "Come, Laura," he said, steering her away. "Let's leave the bridegroom to conquer his nerves and try to survive his last few moments as a single man."

Cole watched them move toward the half dozen folding chairs arranged facing the fireplace. It must have been difficult for them to get away from San Francisco and the family enterprises on such short notice. Their attendance at their only child's wedding was further complicated by the remoteness of Cripple Creek, tucked away as it was in the Rockies with no convenient airport. They'd had to fly into Colorado Springs and rent a car for the drive here.

But they'd made it, arriving less than an hour before the scheduled four o'clock ceremony. Jared and Lark and even baby Gray were here, not to mention the minister. In fact, everyone Cole had invited was here...except the bride.

Damn her! If she thought for a minute that he'd let her get away with this—

The door to the suite slammed open and everyone turned in surprise. For an instant, Jenny stood framed in the arched mahogany doorway. Cole had a quick impression of wild blue eyes...long silky hair crowned by a wreath of flowers...ankle-length, cream-colored gown adorned with lace and ruffles. It was a dress which might be one of her period costumes, he realized, overcome by relief and even able to feel a certain amusement, now that she was here.

And how like Jenny; she carried her shoes in her hand, high buttontops of ivory leather with low wineglass-shaped heels.

Cole's most overwhelming impression was of her loveliness—and how nervous she was. She looked ready to explode into a thousand pieces, all her emotions lying just beneath the surface.

"I'm sorry!" she cried, hurrying into the room. "The time just got away from me." Without looking at anyone but him, she sat down on the nearest folding chair and began pulling on her shoes.

J.C. stopped beside her chair, and Cole saw the child's dark hair was slicked back in that un-natural way favored by the mothers of little boys everywhere.

He looked at Cole with a crooked smile. "I couldn't find my good shirt," he explained, glancing down at his plain red knit. "I'm sorry, too."

Cole felt a possessive surge of feeling toward these two, and he slid his arm around J.C.'s shoulder. "No need to apologize," he said gently. "You're here now. That's all that's important."

And it was, for her appearance, no matter how late, meant only one thing.

He'd won. Now he could relax and claim the prize.

Jenny's decision had not been so very difficult after all.

Perhaps Cole could learn to love her again someday; perhaps not. But she had to take the chance because he already loved his son.

And J.C. needed that love. What more did a mother need to know?

But once she'd made up her mind to go through with it, there'd been no way to avoid being late for the ceremony. That's why she'd ended up with her shoes in her hand and her heart in her throat. That's why she didn't realize at first that there were strangers present.

Now she looked up at Cole, who'd waited patiently while she buttoned her shoes. "I really *am* sorry," she said.

"You're forgiven." He spoke gruffly, offering his hand. "Jenny, before we go on with the ceremony, I'd like you to meet my parents, John and Laura Stadler."

Aghast, she stared at the attractive couple beside him. His parents! What must they think of her?

"Oh, dear." She jumped to her feet. "I didn't know—"

The woman smiled. "Of course you didn't, dear." She ignored Jenny's outstretched hand in favor of a hug. "Welcome to our family."

Her generosity further unnerved Jenny. "T-thank you. That's very kind of—"

"Kind has nothing to do with it," the man, an older version of Cole, interrupted with a smile. "All we want for our son is his happiness."

Cole drew J.C. into the intimate circle. "That's all I want for my... new son, too. J.C., these are your grandparents."

The boy hung back shyly. "Hi," he mumbled, clinging to Cole's hand. He buried his face against his father's side.

"Ahem." The minister cleared his throat. "Since we're running a little late, folks—"

Jenny turned to him. "Reverend Gladstone, if I could have just one more minute to speak to my... fiancé." The word felt strange on her tongue.

"Of course, Jenny." The elderly minister sighed. "But only one!"

She nodded and drew Cole aside. He seemed puzzled but not alarmed. Bracing herself, she forced out words that must be said. "I feel it only fair to tell you that I almost didn't come."

"I'm well aware of that." His dark brows soared. "But you *did* come. That's all that matters."

She pressed her lips together for a moment, bracing herself to go on. "I... just want to remind you that there's still time to change your mind. It would spare us both—" she glanced around the room at the expectant faces "—*all* of us considerable pain. I can't imagine this marriage will be a success, no matter what your parents or my brother—"

"Shut up, Jenny." He caught her by the elbows and lifted her onto her toes for a quick, hard kiss on the lips. When he set her back down, his tawny eyes flashed. "That's your answer."

"Now, now." Cole's father approached, beaming at the two of them. "None of that before the ceremony. Reverend, if you're ready, I think this boy of mine had better marry that girl quick, before she realizes what a rogue she's getting and changes her mind!"

Everyone except Jenny, who knew how close to the truth that innocent remark cut, laughed politely. Even the minister smiled before beginning with the familiar words of the traditional wedding ceremony.

"Dearly beloved, we are gathered here today..."

At Cole's side, Jenny listened with a growing sense of defeat. She was mere minutes away from marriage to the only man she'd ever loved.

If only he loved her in return, her life would be a fairy tale instead of what it was: a tragedy. The sound of Lark, sobbing quietly in the background, provided a counterpoint to Jenny's roiling feelings.

But she had had no choice but to make the best of this impossible situation. Carefully, unobtrusively, she slipped one hand into the pocket of her wedding gown, her fingers closing around the beautiful diamond ring this man had given her so long ago.

She'd almost gone crazy trying to find that ring; it should have been in her jewelry box and not in J.C.'s toy box, which is where she'd finally found it. She'd taken time she couldn't afford because the gesture she'd decided to make seemed somehow important.

When the time came for Cole to slip the wedding band upon her finger, she intended to return the favor with this ring he never expected to see again.

"*May we have the rings, please.*"

"Only one, Reverend."

Cole reached for her hand, found it in her pocket and gave her a quizzical glance. He drew it out, his touch firm. She watched him slip the plain gold band onto her third finger. The ring slid on as if it had been made for her, although she'd not even so much as seen it or tried it on before today. She stared at the symbol of marriage as if mesmerized. Only belatedly did she realize she'd missed her chance to make a gesture of her own until it was too late.

"*I now pronounce you husband and wife. Cole, you may kiss your beautiful bride.*"

The small audience applauded. Cole touched Jenny's chin with a possessive hand, tilting her face toward his for a kiss of carefully controlled passion. Then he kissed her cheek before whispering into her ear, his tone thick with satisfaction, "You're mine, Jenny, all mine from this day forward for as long as we live."

A life sentence of unrequited love, she thought, turning to accept congratulations. Everyone looked so happy, especially J.C. He waited for his chance, then slipped in between his parents.

He slid one arm around his mother's waist and tugged at Cole's elbow. "Are you my daddy for real now?" he inquired into a sudden silence.

The longing in J.C.'s voice made Jenny's heart stop beating. This was why she'd done what she'd done: for her son.

Cole seemed to have trouble formulating the answer he wanted to give. Finally he said, "I've always been your father, J.C.—"

Jenny gasped; surely he wouldn't tell the boy here, in front of all these people.

He gave her a cryptic glance before continuing. "At least in my heart."

John Stadler knelt before the boy, dignified even in that. "And I'm your grandfather—J.C., is it? And this pretty lady—" he indicated his wife, Laura, who beamed down at the boy "—is your grandmother. When your mother said 'I do' a few minutes ago, you acquired an entire new family." He looked up at Jenny. "And so did you, my dear."

She nodded her thanks, feeling the sting of tears behind her eyelids. In the background, sentimental Lark dabbed at streaming eyes while Jared looked immensely pleased with the situation. In fact, everyone looked pleased...but most especially Cole.

Cole Stadler, her new husband; she was Jenny Stadler now. She glanced toward the door leading to the bedroom, then quickly away. She dared not allow herself to think ahead to her wedding night or she'd risk bursting into tears before the ink was dry on her marriage certificate.

Jenny moved through the elaborate reception as if in a daze. Cole, the proud bridegroom, never

left her side. Although this would normally have
made her nervous and anxious, this time she was
grateful. Without his support, she wasn't sure she
could have survived it.

All the hotel employees, all the hotel guests and
many of her Cripple Creek friends, passed
through the receiving line. Jenny shook hands
and offered her cheek for the kisses of well-
wishers over and over again. From time to time,
her gaze sought out her son, who seemed more
than content at a table with his new grandparents, his aunt and uncle and cousin.

In fact, the occasion was quite a festive one;
she'd have enjoyed it, were she not the central
player in this little drama. The ballroom, with its
striped dance floor of alternating strips of dark
walnut and white ash, had always been a favorite
room of Jenny's. The high ceilings were of ham-
mered metal, and a fountain stood in the middle
of the entry, sending sprays of water from the
mouths of fishes held aloft by gilt cupids.

When at last the guests had been greeted and
champagne toasts made to the happy couple,
Cole drew Jenny into his arms for the first dance.
The small orchestra struck up a sentimental love
song while he swept her unresisting form around
the dance floor.

She moved as if in a dream, her feet seeming
to skim independently over the floor. He held her
close in a possessive embrace, pressing her face
so close to his throat above the white collar that
she could feel the heat of his skin without actually touching it.

"You're a beautiful bride," he murmured, looking down at her while sweeping her into a graceful turn. "But I get the very strong feeling that you're not really...here. What is it, Jenny? Is there anything I can do? I tried to make it perfect for you...."

His voice trailed off on a note of disappointment, and she felt a shaft of remorse. "No, everything is fine," she said in a calm voice completely at odds with her true feelings. "You've done a wonderful job and I...I thank you for going to so much trouble."

"No trouble." He frowned as if displeased by her comment.

"You didn't tell me your parents would be here."

"I wasn't sure they'd be able to make it on such short notice."

"Do they...know about us?"

"Not yet, unless they've guessed." His arms tightened around her. "I haven't had a chance to tell them but I will—*we* will. They have a right to know about their grandson."

As Cole guided her in a sweeping turn, Jenny caught a glimpse of his parents and J.C. across the ballroom. She saw the boy's sudden wide grin, heard John Stadler's hearty laughter.

J.C. looked so happy, happier than she'd seen him in a long time. And why shouldn't he be? He'd gained not only a father but grandparents, as well. She should be glad she'd been able to do that for him—*was* glad, in fact. Still, the piper must be paid.

She glanced up at Cole and found him staring at her, a slight frown marring his face.

"What were you thinking about, Jenny?"

"J.C.," she said, which was mostly true. "He seems to be having a good time with your parents."

"Oh." Again, that look of disappointment. "I thought you might be thinking about...us."

"Of course I'm thinking about us, too—how could I help it?" She bit her lip, sorry she'd let him get even that slight rise out of her. "This has been the...strangest day of my life. I don't feel married, no matter what a minister might have said. This entire event—" she glanced around the festive ballroom "—seems like some gigantic hoax. These people are all here to celebrate a lie and they don't even know it."

"Is that how you really feel about it?"

"How else could I feel?" she asked helplessly. "You forced me into this, so what do you expect?"

For a few moments they danced, and then he murmured, "I expect you to be a wife to me...in every way. And I expect you to do what I am prepared to do—put our son's welfare first."

"You think I haven't? That's the only reason I let you—" She stopped speaking to bite her lip. She hadn't intended to rock the boat, at least not now, in the middle of the wedding reception surrounded by family and friends. "I'm sorry," she added in a low voice. "I'm tense, that's all. Surely you can understand."

"More than you realize." The music stopped. "Shall we spend a few moments with my parents? I think they'd like a chance to know you better."

She allowed him to lead her to their table, to receive an enthusiastic reception. J.C. threw his arms around her and gave her a big hug.

"Grandpa says—"

"Grandpa!" She couldn't help responding to the shock of it.

"Can't I call him Grandpa? He told me to."

She recovered sufficiently to smile at her son. "Of course you can. What did Mr.—Grandpa say?"

"That when we visit him in Fran San—San Fran—" He looked across the table for help.

John provided it. "San Francisco."

"Yeah." J.C. nodded. "When we visit him there I can go to the beach and dig sea shells, right, Grandpa? And go to Disneyland and Magic Mountain and all kinds of neat stuff. Can we go soon, Mama?"

Laura leaned forward to pat the boy's hand. "Now, don't rush your mama, sweetheart. I'm sure neither she nor your father have had time to think that far ahead."

Before J.C. could respond, Lark appeared with a smile for everyone. "They've started serving the buffet and I wonder if any of you would like me to bring you a plate? Jared's watching the baby so it'd be no problem. I've got to warn you, though, everything looks wonderful.'' She smiled approvingly at Cole.

J.C. started forward. "I'm starved. Can I, Mama?''

"Of course, honey. I'll come give you a hand—'' General laughter caused her to pause and look around questioningly.

Lark patted Jenny's shoulder. "Brides don't spend their wedding reception filling plates for little boys, even if they are starving to death. I'll take care of J.C., Jenny. You just sit here and chat with your new parents-in-law.''

From the expression on Cole's face, Jenny knew he favored that solution. When Lark and J.C. had disappeared toward the buffet table, he leaned forward.

"Mother, father, I think there's something you should know.''

John and Laura exchanged a quick glance. Then John said, "I believe perhaps we already do.''

Laura smiled. "Cole, did you think we wouldn't know? That boy is the mirror image of you as a child. We don't know how or why you and Jenny—''

"Nor do we care,'' John cut in quickly. "It's really none of our business, why you failed to do the right thing at the time. We're just happy you've found each other again.''

Their generosity burned in the back of Jenny's throat but she couldn't overlook the implied criticism of their son. "Mr. and Mrs. Stadler, I can't let you think—"

Laura looked wounded. "Please, if you can't call us Mother and Father, John and Laura would be fine."

Jenny bit her lip. "I'm sorry. John and Laura, then. I can't let you think—"

Cole slid an arm around her waist and bore down. "I don't think this is the time or the place for that, Jenny."

She glanced at him in surprise. "But I can't let them think you shirked your responsibility to your son," she said. She turned back to her new in-laws. "The truth is, I never told Cole I was pregnant. He found out only when he came to Cripple Creek. Any f-fault in that direction is mine. I...just wanted you to know it wasn't *he* who failed to do the right thing."

Because Cole held her close to his side, she felt him exhale sharply. Apparently he'd thought her about to say something else: perhaps tell his parents she couldn't let them think this was a real marriage, or a marriage that had any hope of success, or any of a dozen other criticisms.

He dropped a kiss on her temple, speaking to the older couple. "That's true as far as it goes. Someday we'll tell you the whole story. For the moment, I think I can speak for my bride as well as myself when I say we appreciate your understanding and support."

"Excellent," John said. "Now that's out of the way—" He rose and gave his new daughter-in-law a sweeping bow. "Could I prevail upon the bride to favor me with a dance?"

And so Jenny danced with her father-in-law, and when he returned her to the table, Jared was there to lead her back onto the floor.

He took her gently into his arms. "I'm tickled to death for you, Jenny," he declared. "I just hope you and Cole will be as happy as Lark and I have been."

She twisted in his light embrace to stare up at him. "I can't believe you'd say such a thing!"

He frowned. "I meant every word of it. What's the matter, you don't think Lark and I have a happy marriage?"

"I know you do. But *you* know how I got roped into this against my will. How you can hold out the slightest hope of happiness is beyond comprehension."

For a few moments, they danced in silence. Then he said, "Cole Stadler is a good man."

"So? He's also a stubborn and possessive man. He wanted his son and decided this was the quickest and cleanest way to get him. While I, heaven help me, let him manipulate me into an impossible situation."

Jared chuckled. "There you go, overdramatizing again. You love him, you have a son by him, you married him. All's well that ends well. Relax and enjoy it, baby sister. You've got to admit, all this isn't half bad." He indicated their surroundings.

Jenny gritted her teeth. Perhaps she could relax and enjoy this if she didn't have something far more worrisome waiting for her later...upstairs...in the bridal suite.

The time had come to go. He'd been generous with her, not hustling her away from the reception early on, but now the time had come and she knew from the look he gave her that she couldn't stall any longer.

Cheeks burning with embarrassment, Jenny returned the hugs of her family members, Lark last of all.

"I left something for you upstairs in the suite," Lark said. "I didn't have time to do all the special things I'd have liked but—"

"Just having you here is special enough." Jenny held her sister-in-law tight. She felt Lark's tears on her cheek.

"Just be happy, okay?" Lark stepped back, swallowing hard. "I know there are...things that still bother you but you'll get past all that. Trust me, Jenny. I know. If Jared and I could find each other, there's hope for you and Cole, no matter what you think."

And then they were separated by gathering well-wishers, opening tiny net bags of the birdseed which had replaced rice in the interests of ecology. Licking her lips, Jenny knelt to hug J.C. "You be good and do everything Uncle Jared and Aunt Lark tell you to do," she instructed.

"Sure, Mom, don't worry!" He kissed her cheek. "Come back soon from that honeymoon stuff, okay?"

"Okay."

Cole lifted the boy off the floor and caught him in a bear hug. "When we see you again, we'll be a real family. Will you like that, J.C.?"

J.C.'s smile was a million watts of happiness. "I like it already!" He gave his father a fierce hug.

Cole set the boy on the floor and turned to Jenny, taking her hand. "Are you ready?"

"F-for what?" She held back.

"We're going out the front door in what will probably be a vain effort to fool everybody, then up the back stairway to the suite." His amber eyes took on a predatory gleam. "Once there, we may not come out for a week. So I repeat, are you ready?"

Jenny sucked in a quick, anxious breath. "As ready as I'll ever be," she said.

He gave her a quick, hard look, then led her toward the door and through the pelting of birdseed.

CHAPTER TEN

ALMOST before the heavy carved door of the bridal suite swung closed behind them, Cole pulled Jenny into his arms.

"I've just been waiting to do this," he murmured, cupping her face in his hands while he stared into her eyes with a question in his which she could not answer.

His kiss betrayed a new intensity. Powerless to resist, she kissed him back. He was sure of her now; she could taste his certainty. He slid his hands sensuously down her throat, over her shoulders, stroked and caressed her body while he took what he wanted from her mouth.

She was lost in the power of the past and the terrifying prospects of the future. His intentions were clear, and why not? She was his wife now, which was more than could be said of the other times they'd been together. The "I do" she'd uttered only a few hours earlier might have been strained but it still represented a promise he intended to collect upon.

He kissed her cheek, her eyes, her temple, then lifted his head to look down at her. He was breathing heavily, but then, so was she.

Stepping away from her, he stripped off his dark jacket and laid it on a brocaded chair. In almost the same motion, he loosened his tie. "I thought we'd never be alone,'' he said with a sigh, tossing the tie atop the jacket. He looked at her and his triumphant expression turned into a frown. "Are you all right? You look…like some kind of virgin sacrifice.''

She forced a laugh. "Which we both know I'm not,'' she said, striving for lightness.

Her attempt at humor seemed to satisfy him for he smiled, then glanced toward the table where the linen-wrapped neck of a bottle rose from a crystal wine bucket. "I ordered a bottle of very special champagne for us to toast our union,'' he said with obvious satisfaction. "That should help you relax.''

Nodding, she turned toward the fireplace, her hands cold as the marble mantel. Behind her, his voice continued soothingly.

"If the ghost stories you told me about this place are true, I expect we'll finally lay old Able to rest tonight.''

"Oh?''

"You said it yourself—from that day to this, no one has ever spent an uneventful honeymoon in this place. Plaster falls from the ceiling, fires start mysteriously, lights go on and off—damn!''

"What is it?'' She turned, alarmed by his unexpected expletive.

He held the bottle of wine aloft. "This isn't the champagne I ordered.''

"It isn't?''

"I wanted you to have the best—and you will.''

"But—" She bit her lip. If he chose to make an issue of the wine, who was she to dissuade him? It would be a kind of reprieve, after all.

He crossed the room and lifted her hand for a kiss. "Why don't you get into something more comfortable while I take care of this little problem?" he suggested.

"All . . . right."

"I won't be long."

"All right."

"Jenny, I—" He stopped short. When she looked at him wide-eyed, he shrugged. "I'm glad we're married. Don't go 'way—I'll be right back."

She stood alone in the middle of the parlor, her heart beating with a heavy cadence. Then she forced herself to turn toward the inner door and walk into the bedroom.

She had never seen a more beautiful room. She stopped short, staring at the massive bed. Lavishly carved of gleaming rosewood, it stood majestically beneath a wooden canopy that supported swags of rich, golden-brown fabric and white netting which cascaded over the satin-and-lace counterpane like a bridal veil.

Apricot-colored rose petals lay in the graceful folds of netting and bouquets of roses were scattered about the room. Jenny loved the perfume of roses. She drew a deep breath, closing her eyes for a moment while she tried to calm her nerves.

When she opened her eyes again, the first thing she saw was the box. It rested on the padded stool at the foot of the bed: a plain white box with an embossed golden logo consisting of a stylized dove and a multitude of hearts. The gift from Lark and Jared, she supposed. Crossing to pick it up, she sat down on the stool and flipped open the lid.

Inside on a profusion of snowy tissue paper lay a note. She picked it up and read, "For you, darling Jenny, on your wedding night. Our love and best wishes are with you always. Jared and Lark." Laying aside the note, Jenny spread back the tissue to reveal a gossamer white nightgown and negligee.

Her fingers closed upon the filmy fabric, crushing its folds. No! She couldn't do this. She couldn't fall into the arms of the man she loved when he didn't love her in return. She had already given him everything else: his son and his way.

This final thing she could not, would not, give on his terms.

Without stopping to think about what the repercussions of what she was doing, she tugged the wedding ring from her finger and dropped it atop the mass of lace and chiffon. She must find a place where she could be alone to think about what she'd done to her life—and what she must do to make things right.

Lifting the skirts of her wedding gown around her knees, she let herself out of the bridal suite and crept down the back stairs, hoping against hope that no one would see her.

There had always been one constant refuge in Jenny's life and that was Wolf Cabin. Even

during the years when ownership was in the hands
of Lark's father, Jenny and Jared had still considered the cabin their birthright. It had been
cause for rejoicing when Jared managed to buy
back what their ancestors had so lovingly created.

In the intervening years, Jared had restored
both cabin and contents to something approxi-
mating its original condition. Now Jenny drove
through the starlit night knowing she was heading
toward the only place where she might be able to
think her way through her predicament. Where
a stranger might have faltered on dark mountain
roads, she drove with the utter confidence of the
native, perhaps as her Ute Indian ancestors might
have ridden their ponies.

At the fork in the road, she turned right,
moving always higher up the mountain. She knew
exactly where to turn off the faint path, even
though the cabin was set well back into the
shadow of trees before a low ridge. She parked
her little car before the porch and jumped out,
breathing deeply of pine-scented mountain air.

She was home. Nothing bad would ever happen
to her here. She could pull solitude around her
and think without the constant pressures exerted
by the expectations and desires of others.

She could consider everything and make her
own decisions here. Throwing back her head, she
stared up at a crescent moon until tears obscured
it.

Dawn was streaking across the eastern sky
above the mountaintops by the time Jenny fell

asleep in a rocking chair on the front porch. Still wearing her wedding gown, she'd wrapped an Indian blanket around her before settling down, for nights in the mountains could get cold during any season.

When she stretched and opened her eyes hours later, the first thing she saw was Cole, sitting on the steps watching her.

Horrified, she leapt to her feet and backed away, the blanket trailing after her. "What—how—you—" She sputtered to a confused halt.

He didn't say a word, just sat there looking at her. He wore jeans and mountain boots and a soft blue sweater, and his forearms were crossed over a raised knee. How long he'd been sitting there, just watching her sleep, she had no idea.

With a moment to catch her bearings, she frowned. He looked tired...and, for the first time since she'd known him, perhaps a bit discouraged.

She chewed on her lower lip, realizing this wasn't the way he'd intended to spend his wedding night: chasing off into the mountains after a reluctant bride. A wave of shame washed over her. She'd acted strictly on impulse, thinking that he wouldn't be able to find her until she was ready to *be* found. Yet here he was already.

Grabbing the long swatch of hair tangling around her face, Jenny twisted it nervously between her hands before tossing it back over her shoulder. "Jared told you where to find me," she guessed unhappily.

Some spark of disappointment flared in his amber eyes. "Jared knew?"

She shook her head. "But he could guess."

Cole shrugged. "I didn't consult him. Come on, Jenny, do you think I went around asking everyone I met where I might find my runaway bride?"

"I guess not," she admitted, "but I don't like being called a runaway bride."

"If the shoe fits."

He sounded so sad, so disappointed, which threw her even farther off balance. Not knowing how to break the increasingly tense silence, she finally said, "Uh...I think there might be a can of coffee inside. Would you like some?"

"I *need* some." He rose smoothly.

She led him inside, through the small living room, past the stairs and into the kitchen. While she busied herself with building a small fire in the wood cook stove and measuring coffee into the tin coffeepot, he simply sat and watched her.

It took all her courage to carry on, but at last she was able to pour two mugs of the steaming brew and carry them to the hand-carved wooden table.

He watched, his face impassive. "Thank you."

"Shall we carry our coffee outside onto the deck?" she suggested, not liking the feeling of confinement in the small room.

"Why not?"

Again she led the way, this time through the back door and onto the deck. Cupping both hands around her mug, she sat down on a wooden stool. "How *did* you find me?" she asked.

He leaned against the railing, staring out at the mountains. An aspen forest crested the eastern ridge but lodgepole pines and ponderosas were beginning to edge out the more delicate aspens. Underbrush bloomed like a wild garden beneath the trees.

He took his time answering. "It wasn't hard," he said at last. "You pointed out this road when we went to tell Jared and Lark our good news. Remember?"

"Vaguely."

"This is a beautiful spot."

That produced her first smile. "Yes. I've always loved it here. This cabin was built by my several-times-great-grandfather, who was a Ute Indian. Each generation added a little or changed a little until Jared put a stop to that. He's determined to keep it just the way it is."

When Cole didn't respond, she hurried to fill the uncomfortable void. "Jared and Lark fell in love here. She was a *real* runaway—from an engagement to another man. When she went back to Florida to marry the guy, Jared went after her and carried her away on her wedding day. It's the most wonderful, romantic story I've ever heard. They've lived happily ever after, as I'm sure you could tell."

He just looked at her with that level gaze, and she heard herself babble on.

"There's a lookout rock back there in the forest, where you can see the entire countryside, and a hot springs a couple of miles over that way." She waved in the general direction. "There's a little waterfall and a natural pool, where we used to swim as kids—"

She stopped talking at last to stare at him, gazing out over the verdant valley below. "Jared says mountains do things to people, whether they know it or not," she whispered. "He says no one can see a mountain without being changed by the experience. Have the mountains changed you, Cole?"

Slowly he turned. "Something has," he said quietly, "but I tend to think it was you, not all this—" He made a sweeping gesture with one arm which included all outdoors. "Magnificent as it is."

"Oh, Cole..." She let her head droop, the curtain of black hair surrounding her.

"No, Jenny, don't try to hide from me. I want to know why you left me on our wedding night."

He had every right to an honest answer. Although he had exerted unmerciful pressure, she'd been the one who'd said *yes*. Swallowing hard, she forced herself to look at him. "It wasn't *our* wedding night, Cole, it was *yours*."

He flinched. "Perhaps it seemed that way, but it wouldn't have been. I would have made it good for you, too."

She groaned. "That's not what worried me— don't you think I know that? It's just..." She closed her eyes for a moment before going on. "Don't you see, this was for the best? Now we can get an annulment."

"Is that what you want? An annulment?"

"I don't see any other way." Her hands were shaking so badly that she set her coffee cup on the deck beside her stool. "I was wrong to marry you, especially after you made your expectations clear. I thought I could go through with it, but I couldn't." She covered her face with her hands, her words becoming muffled. "This wouldn't be so difficult if I didn't . . . care for you so much."

His tone grew sharp. "You have a funny way of showing it."

She dropped her hands into her lap and sucked in a deep breath. She would be honest with him now, if it killed her; *that's* what she had decided in the interminable hours she'd spent searching her very soul. "Cole," she said in a low, weary voice, "I love you. I've always loved you. It's *because* I love you so much that this has become such an impossible situation for me. I could have married anyone else and kept myself . . . *aloof*— kept myself safe. With you, I have no defenses."

He didn't believe her, she realized with sinking heart. He looked at her as if this must be some new gambit for him to figure out. Slipping one hand into a pocket of her bedraggled wedding gown, she pulled out a small, lacy handkerchief and began untying a knot in its corner.

"Perhaps this will help you understand," she said, extending her hand.

He stared down at what lay in the wrinkled corner of the wisp of linen: the ring, the diamond ring he'd given her years before on the cruise ship.

"I was saving it for J.C.," she said simply. "I thought it would be the only remembrance he'd have of his father. When that was no longer the case, I intended to slip it on your finger during the wedding ceremony. When the time came, I just couldn't do it."

He nodded slowly, his expression still under strict control. "You were holding back. I suppose you still are." He lifted the diamond from her palm. "What does this ring symbolize to you, Jenny, that you couldn't offer it to me at our wedding?"

"Love," she whispered. She took the ring from him with hands that trembled, desperate for some reason to have it back in her possession. She had underestimated its importance to her. "If I thought you could ever love me—but you'll never forgive or forget. You've made it very clear that J.C. is your only priority."

"You're dead wrong, Jenny. I *do* love you."

Her head flew back and she stared at him with eyes that burned. "Don't turn into one of those men who'll say anything to get what he wants," she cried.

His sharp laughter shattered what little composure remained to her. "I married once without love," he said. "I'd never do it again, for any reason."

"Not even to gain a son?"

"Jenny, Jenny." He shook his head as if he pitied her. "I didn't have to marry you to get J.C. I've got the money and the power to do any damn thing I want to do, where he's concerned.

I didn't have to marry you to get him—or you, either, if you'll be honest about it."

"Then why? Why did you do it—and force me to do it?"

"I didn't know myself, for a long time. Now I understand it was because...I love you. As you said, I loved you then and I love you now. In between, I despised you in direct proportion to that love."

"You're saying that now to get what you want," she said wearily. "If you'd said it last night, everything would have been different." She stared at him with vulnerable eyes. "I want to believe you but I can't...."

"You held the proof in your own hand." He reached into his pocket and withdrew a plain gold wedding band, the same ring she'd left behind in the bridal suite. "Yesterday—our wedding day— was the happiest day of my life. I knew you were confused and a little angry, but I was sure that once we were alone I could persuade you—oh, hell. You left before I got the chance."

He handed her the ring and she took it unwillingly. "I don't want this," she said, holding it as if it burned her palm. "Please, I left it behind because—"

"If you'd read the inscription inside, I don't believe you'd have gone."

"There's an inscription?" Turning the ring until the lettering inside could be seen, she read the engraved words. *To Jenny: I'll always love you. Cole.*

He watched with a certain amount of resignation. "At the very least, I thought that once I married you, I could love you without worrying that when I turned around, you'd be gone again."

"And then you turned around and I was gone again." Jenny didn't know how she could speak around the joy rising to tighten her throat.

He nodded. "I can't keep chasing you for the rest of our lives, Jenny. It's up to you to tell me what you want. If you want the marriage annulled…" His amber eyes were bleak. "I'll insist on joint custody of our son, but that's the only demand I'll make of you. In return, I'll give you child support and a generous settlement. The choice is yours—hell, the choice should always have been yours. I fought for you the only way I knew how, but the choice was always yours."

She managed a tremulous smile. "I want what I've always wanted but never expected to have— your love." She took a step toward him on shaky legs. "I want *you*, Cole. I've mourned you since the day I lost you. But when you came roaring in here like Hurricane Cole, all I could think of was protecting my son."

"Our son." He smiled and opened his arms.

She walked into them, resting her cheek on his chest. "Our son. You love him, too. I know how much a boy needs his father—and I need his father, too. I love you, my darling. What I want is you—" She choked out a shaky little laugh, her pulse quickening. "You and the honeymoon I cheated us out of."

She felt the tension flow from his body, felt the shudder of strong emotion. "I love you, Jenny Stadler," he said, "and I'll be more than happy to oblige."

He scooped her up into his arms before she knew what was happening. For a moment he stood there on the deck, one arm beneath her knees and the other supporting her shoulders while she clung to him in breathless anticipation.

Suddenly he threw back his head and laughed, the strong cords standing out in his brown throat. "No more runaway brides," he announced. "But I'm all in favor of a runaway honeymoon."

And so was the woman he loved.

Late that afternoon, they left Wolf Cabin for the short drive to Jared's ranch. There they found J.C. helping his uncle feed the horses in the corral.

When they stopped the car and climbed out, the boy ran toward them with joy on his face. He threw himself at them, including both in his embrace.

"Look, Uncle Jared," his muffled voice emerged. "The honeymoon's already over!"

Jared cocked his head, his faced filled with speculation. "I don't think so," he said, humor coloring his tone, "although I've got to agree there's *something* going on here."

Jenny felt her mouth stretch into a smile so broad it made her jaws ache. Here she stood in her wrinkled wedding gown, barefoot, her hair tied back with a piece of string she'd found in the kitchen of the cabin, with her casually dressed bridegroom at her side—and both of them smiling like Cheshire cats.

Yes, Jared could well say *something* was going on.

Lark came down the steps, her smile faltering at the sight of them. "My goodness," she exclaimed. "What's happened? Is anything wrong?"

Cole hugged Jenny tighter, his eyes dancing with amber lights. "Shall we tell them?"

"Let's!" Jenny brushed her lips against his before confronting her astonished family. "I love this man," she announced, snuggling closer against his chest. "Even more amazing—he loves me back!"

Jared frowned. "Well, hell. I knew that."

Lark reached her husband's side. "He's brilliant," she said, slipping her arm through his. "*I'm* the one who told him."

Cole broke into delighted laughter. "You two could have saved us a lot of heartache if you'd let us in on the secret," he teased. "As it was, I had to follow her all the way to Wolf Cabin to find out—"

"Wolf Cabin!" Lark's eyes grew round. "Last night? But I thought— The bridal suite at the hotel— What—?"

"Don't look so shocked," Jenny said, smiling. "I admit, I got . . . well, let's just say an advanced case of cold feet."

Cole chuckled. "No wonder, the way you run around barefoot all the time."

"Get used to it!" Jenny felt confident enough to say anything to him now. "As I was saying, Lark, this brilliant man I married tracked me down and this morning we talked it all out. And then—" She felt hot color stain her cheeks; she'd gone as far as she cared to go with her explanation.

J.C. looked up hopefully. "And then the honeymoon got over and we can all go home," he guessed.

Cole ruffled his son's hair, a smile tugging the corners of his mouth. "Not quite, sport. Then the honeymoon got started and it isn't going to be over for a long, long time—maybe ever. Your mother and I are going back to the Miner's Repose to drink that damned-darned troublesome bottle of champagne whether we want it or not—and maybe put a few ghosts to rest once and for all."

The laughter they shared was intimate and thrilling. But there was something else to be done first . . . something that frightened them both.

Jenny knelt before her son, cupping his chin in one hand. "There's something we want to tell you before we go, J.C.," she said, suddenly serious.

"Okay." He looked warily from one parent to the other.

Jenny swallowed hard. This moment had been coming for such a long time. Now that it had arrived, she was terrified to go on, yet continue she must. "J.C.," she said with the very last shred of her courage, "Cole's your father."

The boy looked confused. "Yeah, I know, 'cause you guys got married."

"No, darling." She placed her hands lightly on his shoulders. "I mean *really*. We knew each other a long time ago, and we fell in love. But things...happened. He went back to his home, and I came back to my home, and then you came along and I didn't know if I'd ever see him again so I—"

She couldn't go on. Cole drew her up to slip an arm around her trembling shoulders. "Your mother is trying to say that you're my very own son, for real." His voice sounded as if it were under enormous pressure.

The fateful moment had come; J.C. had heard the truth at last. Together they stared at him, holding their collective breaths while they waited for his reaction.

For an agonizing moment, he simply stared at them. Then, of all things, he shrugged.

"Yeah," he said blithely. "I know that. That's why my real name's Jared Cole—you think I'm dumb or something? I heard Aunt Lark and Uncle Jared talkin'." Suddenly he grinned. "I always wanted a daddy. Now I got one—" His eyes suddenly widened. "Can I have a pony? Can I? Can I have a pony? Please! Gray's got one and he can't even walk good yet. Say yes, Daddy! Say yes!"

"Welcome to fatherhood," Jared said dryly. "Boy, do you have a lot to learn!"

EPILOGUE

COLE and Jenny Stadler, and their six-year-old son, J.C., were very much a part of Cripple Creek Donkey Derby Days the following June. While Jenny stood at the lower end of Bennett Avenue holding her son by the hand, her handsome husband joined in the generally hilarious efforts to unload wild donkeys from a huge stock trailer and get them lined up across the street in time for the start of the big race.

From past Donkey Derbies, Jenny knew the shaggy little animals were completely unpredictable. One would plunge and snort and struggle to escape, while its neighbor would plant all four hooves and simply refuse to budge.

Jenny and J.C., along with hordes of tourists, laughed and shouted encouragement to the men and women fighting gamely to get the donkeys haltered and at the starting line. But although she cheered along with everyone else, Jenny's thoughts were in turmoil.

Just then, one of the sturdy little animals made a sudden break for freedom. Cole and a half dozen others grabbed the critter, fighting to persuade the spoiled and stubborn donkey to take his place on the starting line. A voice on a loudspeaker exhorted the crowd to cheer on the intrepid "jockeys" trying to subdue the "race donkeys."

"Remember, folks," the announcer intoned, "these donkeys work only two days a year—yes, they get three hundred sixty-three days of independence out of every doggone three hundred sixty-five. You'd think the ungrateful little cusses would cooperate a tad more!"

The crowd laughed and so did Jenny, although she'd heard the same spiel or a variation of it for years. It didn't take much to make her laugh today, though. She'd never been happier in her life; what she felt was pure euphoria.

"Hi, Mrs. Stadler!"

At the cheery greeting, Jenny turned to find a pretty young blond woman and a tall, dark-haired young man smiling at her. It took just an instant to place them: the Mitchells, newlyweds currently enjoying the bridal suite at the completely restored and refurbished Miner's Repose. Chelsee and David, if she remembered correctly.

Jenny returned their smiles. "Nice to see you," she said. "Are you enjoying our Donkey Derby?"

"Oh, yes!" Chelsee clung to her husband's arm. "But we're enjoying your hotel even more. I've never seen anything so lovely as the bridal suite."

J.C. perked up. "Did you meet our ghost?"

Chelsee blinked. "A ghost?"

"Don't worry, he's a good ghost," J.C. said confidently. He turned back to watch his father and the Miner's Repose team wrestling with their donkey, a dirty-white animal with garish brown and dirty black splotches on its sides.

Jenny smiled at the couple's reaction. "One of our local legends," she explained. "Actually, Able—"

"Able?"

"That's the ghost's name, Able hasn't been seen in some time." Not since Cole and I spent our runaway honeymoon there, she didn't add. Now the Stadlers lived in an old Victorian mansion, but they retained fond memories of Able. Both Jenny and Cole hoped they'd been instrumental in helping his spirit find peace at last.

"Hey," David, the cocky bridegroom, declared, "I'd just like to see some ghost try to mess up my honeymoon!"

"*Our* honeymoon, dear." Chelsee smiled up at him sweetly. "I'll let you know if we see anything strange, Mrs. Stadler. Okay?" With a wave of her fingers, the couple drifted away.

Smiling, Jenny turned just in time to see Cole and company dragging their suddenly docile donkey toward her. J.C. jumped up and down in his excitement but she kept a firm hand on his shoulder. Cole had other plans. Before she could protest, he lifted J.C. and swung him onto the donkey's back, where he clung like a cocklebur.

"Cole!" Jenny started forward. "What are you *doing*? That's a wild animal!"

Cole laughed, his warm amber eyes teasing her. "Hey, with five of us hanging on to him, what can one little old donkey do? We've got him seriously outnumbered."

"I don't know—" But when she looked at the delight on her son's face as he clung to the donkey's bare back, she had to smile, even if anxiously.

"You can be next," Cole challenged her. "They tell me that last year, you were the one riding the donkey when the rest of the Miner's Repose team dragged him over the finish line. I'd like to see that, sweetheart."

Jenny slid a protective hand over her still-flat stomach. "I'd be glad to oblige," she said serenely, "but the doctor might not like it."

Her gaze met Cole's in loving intimacy. He raised his brows in question, and she saw the exact instant when the news sank in.

"Jenny!"

Leaping forward, he hauled his wife into his arms. She felt him tremble with emotion, or perhaps it was she who trembled; she couldn't be sure.

"I love you!" They said the words in unison, laughed in unison, and then Cole whispered for her ears alone, "If it's a girl, we'll call her Geneva."

And so they did.

Take 4 bestselling love stories FREE

Plus get a FREE surprise gift!

Harlequin Romance ®
brings you

We are proud to announce the birth of our
new bouncing baby series—Baby Boom!

Each month in 1997 we'll be bringing you your very
own bundle of joy—a cute, delightful romance by one
of your favorite authors. Our heroes and heroines are
about to discover that two's company and three (or
four...or five) is a family!

This exciting new series is all about the true labor
of love...

Parenthood, and how to survive it!

Watch for:
#3443 *THREE LITTLE MIRACLES*
by Rebecca Winters

Tracey couldn't forget the devastating secret that had forced her
to run out on Julien Chappelle four days after their honeymoon.
What she hadn't counted on was that her brief marriage had left
more than memories. A set of adorable triplets who needed
their mom to come home! It seemed Tracey had only one
motive for leaving, and three reasons to stay....

Available in February wherever
Harlequin books are sold.

The collection of the year!
NEW YORK TIMES BESTSELLING AUTHORS

Linda Lael Miller
Wild About Harry

Janet Dailey
Sweet Promise

Elizabeth Lowell
Reckless Love

Penny Jordan
Love's Choices

and featuring
Nora Roberts
The Calhoun Women

This special trade-size edition features four of the wildly popular titles in the Calhoun miniseries together in one volume—a true collector's item!

Pick up these great authors and a chance to win a weekend for two in New York City at the Marriott Marquis Hotel on Broadway! We'll pay for your flight, your hotel—even a Broadway show!

Available in December at your favorite retail outlet.

NEW YORK

MARQUIS

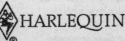

NYT1296-R

You are cordially invited to a
HOMETOWN REUNION

September 1996—August 1997

Bad boys, cowboys, babies. Feuding families,
arson, mistaken identity, a mom on the run...
Where can you find romance and adventure?
Tyler, Wisconsin, that's where!

So join us in this not-so-sleepy little town and
experience the love, the laughter and the
tears of those who call it home.

WELCOME TO A
HOMETOWN REUNION

Sheila and Douglas are going to spend their
honeymoon in a wigwam, by choice. But rumor
has it that Rosemary Dusold may be *forced*—by
runny-nosed babies—to live in one if the new
pediatrician follows through on his intention to
renovate her home as an office. Don't miss
Helen Conrad's *Baby Blues,* fifth in
a series you won't want to end....

Available in January 1997
at your favorite retail store.

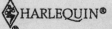

HARLEQUIN®

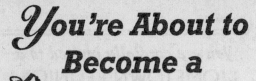

You're About to Become a *Privileged Woman*

Reap the rewards of fabulous free gifts and benefits with proofs-of-purchase from Harlequin and Silhouette books

Pages & Privileges™

It's our way of thanking you for buying our books at your favorite retail stores.

PROOF OF PURCHASE

HR-PP21

Offer expires March 31, 1997

Pages & Privileges ™

TM

Harlequin and Silhouette— the most privileged readers in the world!

For more information about Harlequin and Silhouette's PAGES & PRIVILEGES program call the Pages & Privileges Benefits Desk: 1-503-794-2499

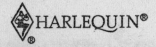

HARLEQUIN®

HR-PP21